THE MYSTERY AT
ROSE COTTAGE FARM

THE MYSTERY AT

ROSE COTTAGE FARM

By Papo

First published in Great Britain in 2011 by

Bannister Publications Ltd
118 Saltergate
Chesterfield
Derbyshire S40 1NG

ISBN 978-0-9566169-4-8

Typeset in Palatino Linotype by Escritor Design
Cover by Design Kabin, Chesterfield, Derbyshire

Printed and bound in Great Britain by the MPG Books Group,
Bodmin and King's Lynn

Contents

Dedication

'The Mystery at Rose Cottage' is my introduction to the world of make believe and mysticism. It is the first in a series of four stories, initially written for my grandchildren. I have introduced them to ancient history and to nature in our countryside, with its abundant variety of wildlife.

The prelude sets the scene. It defines the thinking behind our central character, a most unusual scarecrow.

I based the background to these tales on my romantic vision of what it must have been like living on an idyllic small family farm somewhere in the South West of England. The series develops the imaginary adventures of my grandchildren over a period of years, at the same time posing intriguing questions for the reader to think about.

Dedication and thanks must go to Lucy and William and their mother Victoria. Their encouragement and gentle persuasion helped me create our central character.

My thanks also to Tom Blyth who, with considerable patience and skill, edited and printed this book.

Papo
May 2011

I hear the waves crashing onto the beach,
Grabbing at any grains of sand they can reach.
I see the crabs scuttling in the golden sand,
Scrabbling at coal black rocks they call land.
I hear the pang of a ball as it goes smack on a bat,
I, tripping and stumbling and 'bet you can't hit that!'
Dad reads his book and Mum lies back,
'I want to go home', guess who says that?

Lucy

Map of Rose Cottage Farm

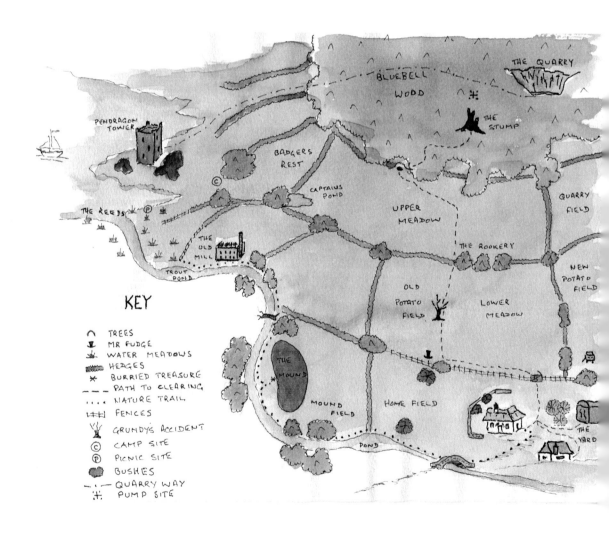

Prelude

Many years ago, more than I would like to remember, there was a little girl, tall for her age with blonde hair and lovely sparkling blue eyes. She was called Lucy Butler and is my eldest granddaughter. She has a younger brother. He has short brownish curly hair and big round brown eyes. He is called William.

Lucy and William lived in a large house with a private drive and extensive garden with lawns and wild grassy fields, somewhere in Warwickshire. They lived happily at Beech house with their Mummy and Daddy, two guinea pigs and a very old gold fish, which had been with them for as long as they could remember.

In the warm summer months they played in their large garden, which Daddy enjoyed cutting in the summer with his 'sit on' mower. Beyond the lawn and tennis court two humpty bumpy sloping grass fields led to a small stream where occasionally, if you were lucky and very quiet, you might just see the occasional small brown fish.

There was a wooden play house and a small den amongst the trees and shrubs, providing everything that two young people could possibly wish for.

Lucy and William had two families of grandparents, still very active. In Lincolnshire, Papo and Mamo lived in a bungalow opposite a large pond always well stocked with ducks.

Living closer to the children were Papo T and Grandma Ruthy, who lived in a lovely old rectory covered in ivy. They had two cats and, in the garden, a family of huge garden snails living under all the decaying leaves amongst the bushes next to the tall red brick wall that surrounded their lovely garden.

When Lucy and William were quite young, Papo started to tell them bedtime stories about an imaginary scarecrow, who, for the sake of a better name, he called Mr Fudge. He and his wildlife friends lived on a small farm somewhere in Dorset. He happened to be a very special scarecrow indeed.

Over the years as Lucy and William grew up, Papo would think up more stories about Mr Fudge. As they evolved they were added to the existing ones and constantly repeated. Over many years other family members made an appearance in the stories, such as cousins Tom and Katie, who came on the scene to swell the ranks and join the fun. There was no stopping Papo.

The stories begin on a caravan holiday in Dorset. Mamo and Papo had decided that they would spend their summer holiday in their super new caravan on a site not far from Lyme Regis. Lucy and William were there too, with their parents.

It was Sunday morning and halfway through their holiday. After breakfast, when the washing up had been finished, and all the dishes put away, and the caravan tidied up, the conversation turned to what everyone was going to do for the rest of the day.

And so our story begins.

William, Papo, Mamo, Lucy

Chapter 1

Hidden Treasure

It was nineteen hundred and something or other. The long cold damp winter with its endless frosts and occasional snow flurries was a fading memory. This year, the late spring had been a welcome sign that maybe there would be a fine summer to brush away the winter cobwebs and to recharge our flagging batteries, so that we could enjoy the warmth and long barmy days, relaxing in the sun and eating delicious ice cream.

Just for a change this year the family had decided that instead of braving abroad with all its associated problems and difficulties, for their well-deserved summer holiday, they would venture to the south west of England. They would explore the wooded green countryside and the old coastal region of Wessex, a part of England that was completely unknown to most of the family.

It wasn't difficult to choose the county of Dorset with its beautiful rural countryside, dotted with quiet charming old world villages, where the homes, built of ancient grey stone and with thatched roofs, are tucked away between tranquil grass covered hills. They do say that dinosaurs once roamed the countryside, where now cows and sheep graze peacefully.

The coastline of rugged grey cliffs and shingle beaches hide the remains of a turbulent ancient past. The multi-coloured cliff faces sweep down from undulating grass fields to the sea below. Beautiful beaches stretch east and west as far as the eye can see on a fine summer's day.

A few miles inland from this rugged coast, hidden by ancient woods and extensive coppices, small family farms nestle amongst irregular sized grass fields bounded by tall overgrown hedges. These are the homes for small herds of dairy cattle and flocks of grazing sheep. Here and there, hidden behind its hedges, you might see a cultivated field growing early flowers and potatoes for the local markets.

Dorset is also well known as a county for its immense range of fauna and flora. There are hunting birds soaring high above the hilltops on warm spiralling thermals, looking for unsuspecting prey on the ground below. On

1

the ground, mammals of all descriptions and sizes inhabit the miles of unexplored woods and hedgerows that criss-cross the countryside. Yet much of this is rarely seen by the summer holidaymakers visiting this part of our island home.

Dorset is also a county full of ancient British history. It was once the home of wild prehistoric chieftains and their family tribes who roamed over the undulating landscape. If you look hard you will come upon mysteriously shaped mounds, tucked away out of sight, hidden by dense woods and hundreds of years of unkempt undergrowth. Look even closer and you might find the craggy remains of a ruined castle, still standing proudly and boasting of past glories. It has been said by some eminent historians that King Arthur and Alfred the Great once lived in these beautiful parts.

On the south west coast, overlooking the English Channel lies the ancient, picturesque fishing port of Lyme Regis, perched halfway up the side of a hill. Its old buildings drop dramatically to a semi-enclosed, stone built harbour. These massive structures have guarded the entrance to the town's inner harbour for the last five hundred years or more. Standing on the outer pier and looking at the harbour through half-closed eyes you can imagine tall-masted frigates of the Royal Navy preparing to go to war against the French or Spanish fleets. In those far off days this harbour, like so many others along the south coast, was England's front line of defence against foreign invaders. However, today there is no requirement to guard the inner harbour, and on a glorious warm summer day it's a different scene altogether, as fishing and pleasure boats rest at their moorings, stays whistling and singing in the breeze.

A few miles inland from the town on a gentle sloping west facing hill, surrounded and hidden by old beech and oak trees is a secluded caravan park for vans and mobile homes. It is here that our road of discovery and adventure begins one summer.

It was Sunday morning and halfway through Lucy and William's holiday with their parents Jack and Vicky staying in a nearby mobile home, everyone met at their grandparent's caravan for breakfast. When the washing up had been finished, all the dishes put away and the caravan tidied up, the conversation turned to what everyone was going to do for the rest of the day. Eventually after a lot of chit-chat Papo asked Lucy and William if they would like to go for a walk with him down to the shore.

"We'll need to put on our strong shoes as the path might be a bit difficult to navigate in parts," he called to them as they rushed off to get ready.

"And don't forget your walking stick Papo," his daughter reminded him, not that he needed much reminding.

Everywhere was as quiet as a graveyard as they walked to the opposite end of the grass field where a few caravans were parked. Passing them quietly, so as not to disturb the owners, they arrived in front of a group of large, ancient, gnarled oak trees, guarding a dilapidated and mostly rotten wooden gate. It was hanging on one hinge and half-hidden in the hedge. It was half open, inviting them to pass through.

The path to the shore

In single file they trampled down the overgrown path with its steep rutted slope covered in lush green grass. Straggly weeds and tall vegetation grew on either side of them, hiding their view. To Lucy it seemed to go on and on for ever and as much as she tried, jumping up and down, it was impossible for her to see either side of the path. Her view of the fields beyond was obscured by tall bushes and shrubs. She wasn't really afraid because William was with her, and anyway, Papo wouldn't do anything stupid, would he?

The sun was shining brightly in the blue sky and the warm air was filled with the sound of insects as the three scrambled and slid down the steep path. After about twenty minutes of energetic effort they came out of the wooded area and found themselves on the grass-covered cliffs. A warm sea breeze drifted up from the beach below. Here and there the smooth skyline was broken by windswept bushes, bending over at a precarious angle on the cliff top.

Except for noisy, inquisitive seagulls flying around, there was no one else in sight. It felt a little spooky being on their own at the top of the cliff with the sea and shore falling steeply below them. The familiar smell of ozone and the

3

sound of the waves lapping up against the shore excited them. Before they knew it, Papo was egging them on to follow him.

"This way guys, follow me," he called out to them as he looked for a way to get from the cliff top to the beach below. In places the scraggy grey cliffs towered at least forty feet above the yellow sandy beach. Unlike the cliffs in other parts of the country, these were jagged and full of small crevices. Each crevice overgrown with small coloured flowers peeking out from the cracks, moving in the breeze that drifted up from the warm sand below them. Lucy just loved the feeling of the gentle warm air caressing her face as she followed William and Papo towards the path.

Lucy shouted out at the top of her voice to Papo that the whole cliff face reminded her of one of her patchwork quilts at home. There were splashes of yellows, interspersed with purples, and blues amongst the green with no recognised order to them, but so beautiful to look at, the whole image shimmering in the breeze.

Black-backed Gull

William was fascinated by black-backed gulls and kittiwakes aimlessly soaring along the cliff face on silent outstretched wings. They were playing follow-my-leader as far as the eye could see, flying out and back again on a never-ending circuit.

"What are they looking for Papo?" he cried out, mesmerised by the sight of so many birds flying together in close formation.

"Anything which might look appetising to eat," explained Papo. The sight of the birds flying effortlessly in the air that rose up from the beach below brought back long-lost memories of when he had flown his radio controlled glider along the cliff face. Then he had pretended to be a gull, joining the soaring birds as they travelled up and down along the cliff face.

As William gazed at the birds, his daydream was interrupted by a shout from Papo. "I think I've found a way down."

They drew closer to him and looked down over the lip of the cliff face to the beckoning rocks below. Then, with the great expanse of the English Channel in front of them, and the smell of the sea in their nostrils, they scrambled and slid down a narrow gully, scoured out by years of rain and wind. They eventually reached the sea shore, huffing and puffing, especially Papo admitted that he was slightly overweight for this kind of adventure.

"Do you know, Papo," said Lucy looking very thoughtful, "I bet smugglers used this path hundreds of years ago to carry barrels of brandy and stolen loot up from the beach at night." In the back of her mind she remembered a story of smugglers' coves and this place suddenly brought it all back to her.

"Don't be silly Lucy," scoffed William, having got his breath back. "It would have been much too steep for them to carry heavy things like barrels all the way to the top."

After a moment's thought Papo interrupted their conversation. "I think Lucy could be right you know. In the days when a lot of smuggling took place along this coast, they used much smaller barrels. A man could easily carry one to the top, even in the dark."

William had moved off and didn't hear Papo's comments. "Come on, let's go this way," He shouted over his shoulder.

He went ahead about fifty yards then stood, barefoot on the shingle beach amongst the rocks. There was a strong, overpowering smell of seaweed and rotting vegetation, mixed in with the sweet smell of the sea. All around him were millions of coloured pebbles, broken shells and bits of driftwood brought in by the tide. The tides were strong along this stretch of coastline and there were so many stories of ships being wrecked on the rocks. They would spew their cargoes on the beaches for the local people to carry away as booty.

Papo and Lucy followed William, their shoes tied round their necks, gingerly stepping around pools of clear sparkling sea water, home to a myriad collection of seaweeds and creepy crawlies. The sand and small pebbles stuck between their toes.

"Look over there," yelled Lucy, pointing to what looked like a cave entrance at the base of the cliff. "It's a cave Papo," she shouted out excitedly, so the others could hear her above the noise of the waves lapping on the sandy beach behind them.

"You're right Lucy," said Papo, struggling to keep up with his two young charges as they scrambled with wet feet over the rocks towards the dark entrance.

"I'm going to put my shoes on before we go another step," he muttered and sat down to dry his feet on a small hanky, before slipping on his socks and walking shoes.

"Come on slow coach," called out an excited Lucy as she approached the entrance, closely followed by her younger brother who was tiptoeing over the pebbles.

"Let's go and explore it, now Papo," she called out as her grandfather made his way up the beach towards them.

"It looks a bit scary," said William hesitantly as he arrived at the entrance, "and it's very dark in there."

"Look, there's a cave over there!"

They stared into the dark entrance, which looked quite menacing even to Papo. He began to have doubts about entering the darkened cave, but Lucy went ahead, because she was brave and William followed her because he was younger. Then Papo followed. He didn't really like caves and the dark, but didn't say anything to the others in case they thought him a bit of a sissy, and no grandfather likes to be thought a sissy, does he?

They had only walked a few paces into the cave when they realised it was quite cold compared to outside and rather damp. It felt eerie and had a pungent, fishy smell. It took a few seconds before their eyes became accustomed to the darkness.

There was some light reflecting on the rock face from the sun coming through the entrance and this allowed them to step carefully into the cave without falling over and hurting themselves. It didn't take long to realise that the roof of the cave was higher than they originally expected and the floor was covered by fine-grained yellow sand that tickled the children's feet and got between their toes.

About thirty feet or so from the entrance and half hidden in the semi-darkness they saw a pool of clear, still water surrounded by smooth rocks that reflected the colour of the cave roof. The water sparkled and shimmered with an array of different colours, red, blue, and green. William thought it looked like all the hues of a beautiful rainbow.

They were just about to turn round and leave, when Lucy stopped in her tracks, and whispered, "Shoosh everyone. Can you hear a strange voice, just over there?" She pointed to the other side of the pool of water that had been admiring. The other two froze in their tracks, not moving a muscle.

"Yes, I can," whispered William, but Papo didn't hear a thing.

"Mamo says you are going deaf Papo," she whispered, and he nodded in agreement, but just then he heard the sound of someone singing. It was a strange eerie song, like an ancient lullaby.

Keeping absolutely still, not even twitching their noses for fear of losing the sound, they listened as the melodic singing filled the cave. Then, with pounding hearts, they lowered themselves onto the sandy floor and quietly inched forward on their hands and knees to hide behind a large rock.

Just beyond the first pool of sparkling water they could just see another, much larger one. The three intrepid explorers slowly lifted their heads to peek over the top of the rock. There, just a few feet away, sitting majestically on a large, smooth boulder was the most beautiful mermaid. She had flowing red hair and green luminous tail, and she swayed slowly from side to side as she sang to herself, her hands smoothing down her long flowing hair.

They gasped in utter amazement, not believing what they were seeing. Was she real, did she exist, or was it just their imagination? Beside her on the floor of the cave, just at the foot of the boulder where she was sitting, and half hidden from view by the sand, was a black wooden sea chest, one corner poking out from the sand. It seemed to her three wide-eyed spectators that the mermaid was guarding it as she sang her sad, wailing song.

"I wonder what she's doing?" whispered William as quietly as he could, fascinated by the sight of this beautiful sea creature, half-human, half-fish.

"Look over there," murmured Lucy under her breath, pointing towards the base of the mermaid's rock. "Can you see that glass bottle sticking out of the sand next to the chest?"

"I can," said Papo, so quietly that he could hardly hear his own words for the pumping of his heart, which echoed in his ears like a large drum. "And I think there's something inside it too. It looks like a piece of paper. Do you think there's a secret message written on it?" Papo, like many people of his generation, had a fertile imagination. "Be quiet you two, we mustn't scare her," he whispered.

"I'd like to know what's inside that chest," said William in a hushed voice.

"Me too," Lucy and Papo said together quietly.

Inside the cave

At that very moment, William turned his head and looked towards the entrance of the cave. His body stiffened with fear as he saw that without any of them noticing, the incoming tide had crept in, sweeping up the beach and into the cave entrance, and they hadn't heard a thing.

"Look Papo, look behind you!" shouted William, jumping to his feet, completely forgetting what they were doing in the cave.

"We must get out of here before the sea cuts us off, or we won't be able to get up the cliff path and back to the caravan." In the same breath he reminded them that no one knew where there were, and if they weren't back for tea they'll have to send out a search party to look for them. William didn't like missing his tea, but he was more afraid of the incoming tide, even though he was a competent swimmer.

The sound of his excited voice echoed around the cave like a ship's fog horn. In a flash of an eye, the mermaid and the chest disappeared from their view. There wasn't even a ripple on the surface of the water in the pool to suggest that she had been there. Where had she gone? Where were the beautiful mermaid and the sea chest?

But it was the incoming tide and their safety that concerned them now, as Papo and Lucy hurriedly got to their feet, Papo looking around for his walking stick on the sand where he had been kneeling.

"Come on, this way kids, follow me," he shouted, "we can't go out the way we came in; the water is far too deep. We better see if we can get out of the cave by going farther in, where the high tide won't reach us." He knew it was a gamble and would be risky, but he couldn't think of anything else on the spur of the moment and time was running out. The sea was getting closer to them and they were now feeling a little scared, even though they didn't want to show it as they scrambled as quickly as they could over the rocks and away from the fast encroaching tide.

It was as black as night inside the cave and they began to fear that they were trapped but as they climbed higher, the noise of the sea became fainter, which they hoped meant that they were out of danger. Papo's immediate thoughts were how long they would have to wait before the tide turned and they could retrace their steps to the entrance and back to the cliff path to safety and home.

Then Lucy, who was leading the climb, saw a speck of light ahead of her. Could it be the sky, she thought as she scrambled towards it, or maybe it was her imagination playing tricks with her in the darkness.

"I can see a faint speck of light up there ahead of us, come on," she shouted eagerly to the others below her.

Although she and William were becoming a little tired Papo's legs were aching with the effort of climbing over the rocks and boulders. Now he could see the light in the distance, but he had to stop for breath every few minutes. As he climbed upwards the light, helped by William and encouraged by Lucy's constant chatter, the speck of light became bigger and bigger, until what they thought was a speck of sky turned out to be a hole, just big enough to squeeze through and out into the cool fresh breeze and sunshine.

Papo who had the most difficulty getting out of the hole, but with pulling from William and encouragement from Lucy, he managed to squeeze through without hurting himself. They were covered in dust and smelling rather pooish but there were big grins on their hot, grubby faces when they found themselves in the open.

"I've never been so pleased to see daylight," wheezed the exhausted grandfather as they flopped on the grass, gulping in of the fresh sea air.

"Me too," agreed the others.

What they hadn't known as they crawled through the hole was that they had just climbed through an old badger's set. It had been abandoned by its owners some time in the past but it retained the sour, rank, stale smell that is typical of badgers' sets. It was hidden from view by a screen of small wind-blown bushes with prickly leaves and branches, and to one side of it stood a solitary hawthorn tree.

The badgers' set

"Thank goodness the badgers weren't here to greet us," said Papo as he rearranged his clothes, using his dusty hands to smooth down his hair. "Maybe this is their summer home and they haven't arrived yet," he suggested. "Anyway, after our rest I think we should make for home, just in case they turn up. You never know, badgers can be dangerous animals if cornered, even though they normally keep away from humans."

"No wonder it was so hard to climb up through the cave from sea level to here," said William. Now that he and Lucy had recovered, they were keen to get home. As they stood at the entrance of the set, with the sea below them, they could make out a wood in the distance that looked vaguely familiar.

"I know where we are," called Lucy, pointing towards the path they had used to get to the cliff top earlier in the day.

William got up, no longer afraid that they might be in danger. After all, it was thanks to him that the three of them had got out of the cave so quickly, and he felt particularly good about that. Wait until Dad hears about it, he thought to himself. He looked at Papo, "What's that in your hand Papo?"

"It's the glass bottle with the message in it that we saw in the sand near the chest," said Papo with a smile. Lucy thought that he looked much happier now that the ordeal was over, thanks to her keen eyesight and William's helping hands.

"I noticed it was still in the sand after the mermaid had disappeared, so I snatched it up as we left the cave. If there is a message, it might tell us more about the chest and the mermaid. On the other hand, I suppose that it might just be something thrown into the sea by a holiday maker."

"Can I see it please?" said Lucy, getting quite excited at the thought of reading a message written by someone else, and then thrown into the sea in the hope that it would reach some distant shore.

"Of course you can" said Papo, handing her the blackened and

The message in the bottle

encrusted bottle. Looking through the murky glass she could just make out the dark paper inside, rolled up like a scroll. She held it up to the sun.

"Shall I take it out and see if there is still writing on it?"

"Yes of course, if you can get the cork out" replied Papo.

"I think it's been a long time in that bottle from what I can see, maybe hundreds of years" William said with a big grin.

"You know it's likely to be stuck hard, Lucy," said Papo, "and we might have to wait until we get back to the caravan before we can get it out."

"Hold on, I have my penknife with me," said William, pulling it out of his pocket. "This should do it, if anything can."

Lucy handed William the bottle and she and Papo watched as he prised out the cork with the tip of the large blade of his knife, careful not to snap the blade or break the cork. Surprisingly, the bottle was still very dry inside after all the years it had probably been in the water and the cave. As he turned the bottle upside down, the scroll of very old, yellowish, dry paper dropped out onto the grass. Papo picked it up and carefully unrolled it so as not to tear it.

They stared at it for a minute or two without touching it.

"This could be parchment you know," he said.

There was some writing on it but it was so faded they could hardly make out the words. At first it didn't make sense, until Papo realised that the writing was in old fashioned English. It read:

You will find me if you look
In Rose Cottage Farm by the brook.
Follow my map and you will see
That I've shown you where the bridge will be.
Cross the bridge and down the path
To the old thatched cottage, home at last.

"Papo, look on the other side," said Lucy. Turning the delicate parchment over in his hands, Papo could just make out a faded, crudely drawn map.

They began to realise that what started had out as a gentle Sunday afternoon walk along the sea shore was turning into something rather special, maybe even an adventure.

Lucy's heart beat faster as her excitement grew. The parchment looked very old. Could the ancient poem and the map be telling them about buried treasure? Would there be a pirate's haul of gold and precious gems?

As they made their way slowly up the path and back to the caravan park they chatted about the message and the map.

"Where do you think Rose Cottage Farm is Papo?" asked William, because none of them knew, nor had even heard of a Rose Cottage Farm.

"I wonder where we start looking?" said Lucy with a frown on her face as she led the way up the path towards the oak trees and the battered wooden gate. The thought of buried pirate treasure took her breath away. Just finding a message in a bottle was fun, but finding one so old was unbelievable. It was something she had only read about in adventure stories. Now it was really happening to her, right now, right here on their holiday!

Half an hour later three exhausted but happy explorers arrived back at the caravan after their surprise adventure in the cave. They flopped down into the easy chairs and began to tell their story to the rest of the family. At first, nobody really believed them until Lucy stood up and proudly showed them the bottle and the scroll inside. Then everyone believed her.

That evening after a mouth-licking supper of fish and chips with lots of tomato sauce, and with the family sitting under the caravan awning, the only topic of conversation was Rose Cottage Farm. The big question was, as Papo explained to everyone, where was it situated?

Hidden treasure?

"No one knows if it even exists today," he said, "and what if the bottle had travelled hundreds of miles to finish up in the cave. The farm might be in another land altogether and not here in Dorset."

Turning to his father, William asked, "Do you think it could have floated across the Atlantic?"

"It might have done, William" was his reply, and for the first time that evening he was beginning to show some interest in their story, although in the back of his mind he thought it was a bit far-fetched. However, what they all agreed was that the puzzle to find Rose Cottage Farm would be another important adventure. They could all join in and there were still seven more days before they had to pack their cases and make for home. That should give them plenty of time to do some detective work, which would be fun!

"We must find it, you know," said Daddy after supper as he unfolded a large motorists' map of Dorset and spread it on the green table. Although it was getting late there was still plenty of daylight left to see the map clearly. "Remember what the poem said and the shape of the map on the back of it. There's no harm if we start to look inland from the coast near here, is there?"

They stood in a circle round the table, looking at the map for the features they could had made out on the old map in the bottle: a stream running through a valley, a bridge over it and a farm building at the end of a long farm track. It was unusually quiet under the caravan until Papo suggested that Rose Cottage Farm might be near to this part of the coast, because the sea currents would have washed the bottle into the cave after it had been thrown into the water.

"We know that" chorused the others," but what we don't know is, where it was thrown in, in the first place!"

Ignoring their cheeky comments he went on, "And another thing, I don't think it was in the water very long before being washed up into the cave."

"Why do you say that Papo?" asked Lucy, thinking about their afternoon experience, how quickly the tide had entered the cave and how frightened she had been at the thought of not getting out.

"Well, there are so many treacherous rocks along this coast line that the chances of the bottle not being broken on one of them are very remote. I'd say that it might have been thrown into the sea from a boat out in Lyme Regis bay before being washed into the cave by the incoming tides. Maybe it was during a winter storm when the tides are higher than in the summer and few people would have visited the cave."

"You know that seems very sensible and quite logical" said the children's father after giving it some thought and not coming up with a better suggestion himself. "Let's look nearer to this area around Lyme Regis," he suggested.

Two hours later it was beginning to get dark and the light was no longer bright enough to pick out the fine detail on the map. They hadn't found the farm and it was getting near to bedtime, but tomorrow they could spend more time on the quest, perhaps inspecting other maps of this part of Dorset.

Papo was the first to get up from the table to stretch his aching legs. "Folks, I'm jolly tied after such an exciting and exhausting day, I'm off to bed. See you at breakfast everyone," he said, stepping into the caravan and leaving the others to tidy up. "Come on Mamo, time for your bed too. I'll fill your hot water bottle for you." Papo did this most nights, because even in summer it can get quite cold in a bunk bed with only a thin mattress to lie on, even though they slept in sleeping bags.

Papo called out through the caravan door as he disappeared, "Lucy and William, don't forget we need your help nice and early at breakfast in the morning please. Same as usual, is that all right with you two?"

No one watches TV on holiday; it's pleasant to have a rest from all the troubles and stresses of everyday life, so no one heard the weather forecast for the next day.

During the night heavy black clouds rolled in from the sea bringing warm rain that fell heavily, rattling loudly on the caravan roof. The rain was accompanied by strong winds that shook the awning to the point that Papo nearly got out of his warm bed to inspect it. The next morning a quick look round both the caravan and the awning confirmed that all was safe and no damage had been done during the night.

Mamo spoke to Vicky on the mobile phone and it was decided that because it was still raining they would spend the morning sitting in their lounge, rather than under the caravan awning. They could study the map in peace and quiet and there would be more room to sit around and spread things out. "Tell Lucy and William not to bother coming to us this morning. We'll come to you for a change," and she rang off.

As soon as they met they agreed that after yesterday's excitement in the cave and the evening's chatter about the message and map in the bottle, they would have to look further afield. Daddy had bought two new maps of Wessex from the caravan site shop and now with three maps they could look for Rose Cottage Farm in earnest.

Daddy was actually very good at map reading, being an airline pilot. He suggested that he should divide the map into squares and give each person a set of squares to examine. Then he showed everyone what to look for. What a bridge might look like on the map, the shape of a lake, a winding stream, and a main road and a farm track.

Mamo would keep everyone occupied until the rain stopped and the weather cleared. She had decided that there were enough bodies crowded around the table so went off to chat and get the lunch ready. However, Lucy's mother was only happy when she could creep into the lounge and look over everyone's shoulders and make suggestions, as mothers do.

They all concentrated hard on their map squares. There was absolute silence, which surprised the adults, and it was nearly an hour later when Lucy suddenly broke the quiet and shouted out, "I've found it! Well, I think I have found it. Look everybody!"

They got up and crowded round her. She pointed to a blue patch in one of her squares. "I think that's the lake, there," she said excitedly, "and isn't that the stream or a river meandering across the meadows, and I think that's the bridge, Daddy, and isn't that thin line a farm track? And do you think that small square just there is where Rose Cottage might be?" She pointed to the image on the map near a bridge sign.

You could feel the excitement in the room as the adults peered over the shoulders of the two children. There were many questions to be asked, but everyone agreed it was pretty likely that she had found the farm, about twenty miles from their Caravan Park, and about six miles inland from the coast.

"Let's go and find it now!" cried out William, unable to control his enthusiasm. There was so much babbling going on that no one heard their Mother summon them for lunch.

"Lunch time everyone," she called again. "You can all wash your hands. Put the maps away now, please, and we'll think about going out in the car this afternoon if the rain has eased up."

Lunch was a very hurried affair but, as usual, very enjoyable. Everyone tucked into pieces of cold chicken and Grantham sausages, which were Dad's favourite, a mixed salad liberally dressed with olive oil, fresh crusty bread and butter, and loads of pickles and sauces for William and Papo.

It was a mad rush to wash the dishes and tidy up, done to a chorus of chatter and laughter. Luckily the rain had stopped and the sun was quickly drying out the short grass around their home. A few rabbits had ventured out from below the homes for a bite to eat.

"Anyone want the toilet? Coats on everyone and into one car, now," said Daddy emphatically. There was a mad scramble for seats. Mamo and Papo were squeezed into the back of the Volvo.

"Seat belts on, have you got the map?" shouted William, and then they were off on another adventure, hoping to find the mysterious Rose Cottage Farm. They weren't sure if it existed but they all agreed it was going to be fun looking for it.

As Lucy had originally found the site on the map, it was agreed that she should be allowed to be their navigator. They drove out of the caravan park and followed the route that Lucy traced with her finger on the map as she listened for her father to mention the signs that he knew would appear on the map. After about half an hour following the A35 main road north of Lyme Regis, not travelling too fast in case they missed anything, she shouted out suddenly, making her father brake quicker than normal.

"Turn right at the next cross roads please Daddy," she called out with delight as the others in the car craned their necks to see what was happening outside. Turning into a narrow road he followed it for a few miles as it twisted

between dense woods and small fields with their high hedges on all sides. The others murmured that they might be lost.

"Don't be silly Mamo," reacted Lucy, "we're following the map, and it says we have to go down this road for a few more miles yet."

They followed the map exactly as Lucy directed. After what seemed like ages, looking out for clues as to where they might be, she saw a wooden signpost sticking half out of the hedge on the left hand side. It was covered in flowering brambles, but to her joy she was able to make out the faint lettering, 'To Rose Cottage Farm'. The sign pointed down a narrow farm track that obviously hadn't seen much traffic over the last few months. Jack stopped the car.

"Well done Lucy," Mummy said after everyone had calmed down. "Do you think this is the Rose Cottage Farm that was mentioned in the scroll?"

"I hope it is. It's got to be," said Papo from the back seat. He was beginning to get that excited feeling in the pit of his stomach at the thought of finding the place that had been written about on the parchment in that bottle, maybe hundreds of years ago.

Jack eased the car off the road and on to the narrow lane. The track was just wide enough to get through without scratching the sides of his car and he drove slowly, looking out for the ruts and dry holes in the surface which had been scoured out by the previous winter's rain. It was evident that very few vehicles used the farm track and he felt that there might be nothing at the end of it. It would be so disappointing for the children if it turned out to be a dead end.

They arrive at Rose Cottage Farm

After what seemed like ages, driving slowly in second gear down the track, the car emerged on to more open ground and they could see fields again. Ahead of them was an old stone bridge straddling a meandering stream, just wide enough to take the width of a car or a small tractor.

Clever old Lucy had guessed correctly and had led them directly to their destination. Just beyond the bridge, standing on the left and surrounded by a large garden, was an old thatched cottage with a solitary red chimney. There were red and yellow roses in full bloom, climbing wildly over the front door and the two front windows. It was a beautiful sight and such a surprise too, for none of the family had experienced anything like it before. As they drove across the bridge, William pointed out a smaller, modern building with a grey tiled roof on the right, and just beyond that, a Dutch barn with some round wheat stacks standing in front of it. The scene reminded Papo of some of the farms that he had worked on when he was a student many many years ago, long before he went to agricultural college. This was turning out to be an adventure way beyond what they could have imagined when they found that bottle in the cave.

There was no one to be seen moving about the farm. The yard was deserted, except for a few circling swallows. They parked the car by the new building. Lucy climbed out first and stood on the dry dusty ground. No one said a word. The only sound that broke the silence was the high screeching of the swallows as they swooped down to suck up muddy water from a puddle left from yesterday's rain.

They didn't have to wait long for someone to appear. The back door of the cottage opened slowly and out walked an elderly man. He wore a flat cap and small round glasses that perched on the end of his nose. He was dressed in an old sports jacket which had seen better days. On his feet he was wearing black welly boots.

"Who are you?" he called out rather gruffly as he approached the car. He was a little concerned because very few people ever came to visit him at the farm, especially in a big red Volvo estate car.

Bravely walking up to him, Lucy said in her grown up voice, "Excuse me, I'm Lucy and this is my brother William, and over there in the car are Mummy and Daddy and our Mamo and Papo." Lucy pointed towards the Volvo.

"Oh yes, so why are you all here and what do you want?" he said, sounding not quite so gruff this time as he warmed to the sight of young Lucy, admiring her confidence.

"Please sir, it's a very long and complicated story, but we had to find a Rose Cottage Farm because it was mentioned in a poem written on a scroll which we found in a bottle washed up in a cave," she said in one long breath.

"A scroll, a scroll in a bottle washed up in a cave. Well, bless my soul," he replied, scratching his head under his cap. Jack got out of the car and walked up to them.

Mr Grundy

"Good afternoon sir, I'm Jack, their father." He offered an outstretched hand and the two men shook hands. Jack could feel the farmer's strong grip. He started to explain why they came to be parked in the farm yard. "I hope we're are not causing you any problems, but yesterday, Lucy and William were exploring along the beach, not far from Lyme Regis, with Papo, that's Lucy's grandfather, over there in the car. They found a cave, went in and, believe it or not, they found a mermaid guarding a half-buried sea chest. Buried in the sand nearby was a bottle with a message in it. I know it sounds a bit far-fetched, but it happened."

"Well bless my soul," repeated the old farmer. "What did that strange message say then?" He was showing more interest now and a craggy smile creased his rugged face. With that, William who had been standing next to his father handed the bottle to him.

"Well well, would you believe it?" he mumbled to himself as he turned it over in his hand. "I think you better all come inside." Walking in front of them he turned and said to Jack, "Oh, by the way, my name is Grundy and this is my farm, Rose Cottage Farm. I expect you've guessed that already as you've found your way here."

With the introductions over and now feeling more relaxed, Lucy waved to the others in the car to get out and follow her towards the cottage. Mr Grundy led them into his home, through the large old fashioned kitchen and into what looked like a room kept for special occasions.

"Come this way, come into the front room and we'll have some tea when my wife comes in. She's just feeding the chickens. We keep a few in one of the fields over there," he said, pointing towards one of the windows. "They're for our own use, mind you, and that damned old fox, which is a most unwanted visitor."

They followed him into the cottage, making sure that Daddy didn't bang his head on the low beams in the hallway, something he always does in houses that have low beams like this one.

Mrs Grundy appeared with a basket of brown eggs. She gave them a scrumptious farm tea with freshly baked scones, still warm from the oven, and piles of cream. There was real unsalted butter spread thickly over each half and filled to overflowing with homemade strawberry jam, and there was a lovely fruit cake to finish off the feast.

Daddy stood up, carefully so that he would not hit his head on the ceiling and thanked Mrs Grundy for being so kind to the complete strangers who had turned up unannounced. He promised that they would come back soon to look round the farm and discuss the instructions on the scroll. In the meantime, would Mr Grundy think about the message very carefully and what it might mean?

Mr Grundy was intrigued by the idea of an old sea chest in the cave and the appearance of a mermaid, and what they might mean. Why Rose Cottage

Farm was mentioned in that poem and why did the chest and the mermaid disappear from view? And why were only the bottle and its message left?

What he didn't tell these visitors was that their story wasn't exactly a surprise to him. In the back of his mind there was a niggling thought, and he had to sort it out before they all met the next time, whenever that was going to be.

"Why don't you all come back in a few days and we'll have another chat about the sea chest and the message, and you can look round the farm if you like. If it looks to me that there is some truth in this story and there is something that's worth looking into, then we'll go from there." He smiled to himself as he walked with them across the yard towards their car.

"What a good idea," said Papo, who had been watching Mr Grundy during tea and their subsequent conversation. He thought as he watched the old farmer that there was more to his comments than he was giving away, and he meant to find out what it was.

They all happily agreed that they would revisit the farm in two days, which would allow them just five more days at the caravan park before the holiday ended. There were still other places of interest they wanted to visit and, of course, there were other things to do as well during a summer holiday by the sea.

The next two days sped by with a visit to the harbour accompanied by a fish and chip lunch, swimming in the sea. The children enjoyed splashing in the waves but the grown-ups found it just a little too cold, especially Mamo who only liked to swim in lukewarm water. They also visited the local museum with its fascinating history of the town and harbour. They learnt about the lives of local families who lived in many of the old buildings that were still standing in the town.

The family returned to Rose Cottage two days later, but to everyone's dismay Mr Grundy was not able to throw any more light on the mystery. However, he showed them around his farm, noticing that William was particularly keen on the old tractor in the Dutch barn and the other farm implements stored nearby. His obvious keenness pleased Mr Grundy enormously. What the family didn't know – and why should they – was that he had not had a young lad on the farm during all the years that his wife and he had lived at Rose Cottage. He thought that William showed promise in all types of machinery, and that was good in his eyes.

During the months that followed, Lucy and William took it in turns to write letters to the Grundys nearly every week, telling them about their school, what they did at the weekends, about their friends, and how much they both missed Rose Cottage and the farm. As the letters passed this way and that, the children became more and more friendly with Mr Grundy and his wife, and it wasn't too long before the children were invited to visit the farm, when holidays permitted, of course.

So it was that after that very first visit with the family, others soon followed whenever school holidays and family commitments allowed. Much of their spare time was spent at Rose Cottage Farm, eagerly learning about the mysteries and disciplines of country life and at the same time making some quite extraordinary new friends.

Mr and Mrs Grundy soon began to feel that William and Lucy were the son and daughter they never had. They looked forward to their visits and spoilt them too much. They made the new building into a 'home from home' for the two young people. Bunk beds were bought, a new carpet was laid in the bedroom and matching curtains were hung to make the room comfortable and homely.

Lucy and William loved their visits to Dorset, going there as often as their daddy could spare the time to drive them down from Warwickshire. Soon they would be old enough to use the train, but not quite yet.

Chapter 2

Mr Grundy Has a Brilliant Idea

Deep in Dorset's rolling countryside, miles from any town that you could possibly call a town and at the end of the long twisting farm track where William and Lucy and their parents first met Mr and Mrs Grundy at Rose Cottage, there is a potato field.

It's quite a large potato field compared to many other potato fields in this part of the county. The rich crumbly loamy soil warms up early in the spring, making it ideal for growing varieties of early new potatoes. These 'earlies' as they are known can be harvested before the 'main crops' that are grown in the Midlands and therefore get better prices at market. If it's a good year with not too many late frosts and if the rain comes at the right time, it will always mean good yields for local farmers like Mr Grundy, if they can harvest them early.

Unlike the fields of bigger farms in other parts of the country, with their neat, straight, well cut hedges, this field has overgrown hedges. They surround it on three sides to protect it from the harsh winds that can spring up without warning to catch the unwary. The old hedges also provide ideal homes for nesting birds in the spring, such as blackbirds and thrushes. In the hedges wild brambles covered with huge black juicy berries offer a continuous feast for birds and other wild creatures.

When you stand at the north east corner of the field and look across Upper Meadow, you will see a dark menacing wood, full of old decaying trees. Amongst the rotting trunks you could make out some smaller, younger trees, struggling to grow in the dense undergrowth. There are tangles of huge, broken branches that lie twisted on the ground, where they provide secret homes and hiding places for many of the smaller animals and insects that thrive in these dark surroundings. Throughout the year small furry mammals like field mice and shrews, and larger ones like badgers and foxes, live side-by-side with an incredible variety of beetles and spiders and other creepy crawlies.

If you walk through the wood and crane your neck upwards, you will see that many of the younger, taller trees have high intertwined branches. In summer they are covered in a rich canopy of green leaves of all shades, swaying and whistling in the wind like a ghostly orchestra. This high canopy provides nesting sites for the larger birds like crows and wood pigeons and also a safe home for families of grey squirrels.

In the spring the ground all around and between the trees is carpeted, as far as the eye can see, with brightly coloured bluebells, each clump guarded by a mass of glossy dark green leaves. That's how this wood gets its name, Bluebell Wood.

Very few walkers ever venture here because it is isolated from any road or footpath and few people would want to try to penetrate the dense woodland floor. The local gossip recalls that strange noises have been heard at certain times of the year that no one could explain. There are other things that can't be explained, such as why in over a thousand years there are areas of this wood where the bluebells have not colonised the wood floor. Instead, white nettles grow in profusion and long grass provides a carpet of tall vegetation, void of any colour in the spring. These are places that are home to grass snakes and many other wild creatures that have no fear of man.

Noisy Black Rooks fly in a raucous crowd

Between Upper Meadow and Lower Meadow and near to a gap in the boundary hedge there is a stand of beech trees, which may be two hundred years old. Every year a flock of black noisy rooks returns to nest in these trees, safe from foxes and other predators that live below, on the prowl during daylight for a quick snack. The rookery had been there since Mr Grundy was a young boy; as long as could remember. Most mornings or afternoons the rooks would fly down into the potato field in a raucous crowd to feed.

If you look carefully while the flock is feeding on the crop, you will see that there will always be one or two older birds on the fringe, keeping a watch out for strangers, human or animal. The birds happily peck and feed around Mr Grundy's new potatoes, digging into the soil with their sharp beaks for worms and grubs and anything else that might take their fancy. Their digging disturbs the young growing potatoes, causing the damage that so infuriates Mr Grundy.

The potato field is just one of many small fields belonging to Mr Grundy that make up Rose Cottage Farm. During the spring and early summer months he inspects his valuable potato crop almost every day; sometimes before starting other jobs around the farm, or in the afternoon after lunch, instead of indulging in his regular 'snooze'.

Seeing the noisy rooks on the ground between the rows of young potatoes makes his temper rise and the hair on the back of his neck stand on end. It doesn't matter how often he shooshes them away, as soon as his back is turned, down they fly from their high perches as if nothing had happened to disturb them. But this year he decided to do something to scare those wretched birds away for good.

One warm morning after visiting the potato field, he trudged back into the kitchen for his 'piece' with a worried frown on his face. Something is up, thought Mrs Grundy who was up to her arms in flour, baking bread, and sure enough, he turned to her and announced, "I have decided to make a scarecrow, the best one you've ever seen."

"How nice dear," said his wife quietly, not moving her head. She had heard her husband's complaints about the rooks many times in the past few weeks, but she had done so for many years and knew that it was unlikely that anything would ever happen. She particularly remembered similar 'grand plans' last year and the year before that, so she worked at the ball of dough in her hands, taking no more interest in her husband's outburst.

The silence in the kitchen was disturbed only by the noise of her large hands kneading the dough. After a while she asked, "When are you going to make it then dear?" with the knowing smile on her face that she always wore when she wanted to tease him.

"Right now!" he declared, his voice raising a little. "I'm going to start this morning."

So, as she split the kneaded dough and placed each half into the bread tins, Mrs Grundy knew that this time he actually meant it.

"To start with, I'll need to find a straight pole for his body, about five feet long. Then two pieces of wood and some string for his arms. Maybe I'll use some of that orange binder twine that's lying in the corner of the Dutch barn. It won't rot in the winter. I'll pad out his body using some fresh straw from one of the stacks and I'll look for some old clothes. And I'll give him a big hat."

"That sounds lovely dear," his wife's words softened as she kneaded more fresh dough in the huge brown and white bowl that she had used ever since she got married. "Would you like me to find some old clothes for you, there'll be plenty in your cupboard, I'm sure of that."

"You can't use any of my clothes," he protested. Like all men who grew attached to their jackets and old trousers, he suggested that there might be older ones in the attic that he had no more use for. "I'll have a look up there when I've finished this mug of tea."

Sipping the warm sweet tea and soothed by the familiar aroma of baking bread, he relaxed in his favourite chair in front of the Aga, pondering the task ahead. "I know just the place to find a straight pole long enough for this job", he murmured to himself. "I'll go to Bluebell Wood tomorrow and I'm sure I'll find the tree that I saw recently, with some beautifully strong, straight branches near to the ground."

Turning to his wife, he asked, "Could you please find me a well-rounded turnip for his head and a long shaped carrot for his red nose? As for the sticks for his arms, I'm sure I'll find some in the wood shed." As he sat thinking about the project he was warming to the challenge and was quite excited at the thought of the scarecrow, whose image he had now clearly sketched in his mind. Whether it would turn out as he hoped, couldn't be sure –he would just have to wait and see.

"My dear, don't forget he will need eyes too," said his wife as she washed her hands, dried them on a towel and went to put on her coat before going out to the shed. She thought that if she couldn't find an especially large turnip, she'd have to buy one. It was now obvious that her husband was serious about this scarecrow business, so she decided to go along with the idea for now. You never know, she thought, he might forget about it tomorrow and he'll think of something new. Mrs Grundy was not going to waste too much time hunting for odd bits and pieces of clothing just yet.

It took Mr Grundy two whole days to find all the wood and other pieces he needed to make his scarecrow. He wanted it to be as lifelike as possible, so he took his time, carefully assembling all the parts, before dressing it in some dirty old clothes and a battered black hat that Mrs Grundy had found in the attic.

Luckily she remembered she had seen the hat and the old clothes years ago when her husband had been looking for some old maps of the farm. If she hadn't remembered them, she might have had to use some of Mr Grundy's newer clothes and that would not have pleased him one bit.

"We'll call him Mr Fudge"

At last the job was completed and Mr Grundy propped him up against the back door of the cottage, stepped back two paces and admired his latest creation. He grinned from ear to ear, thinking, I've done a really good job. Indeed, it was a beautiful scarecrow and he was very proud of it as it stood against the wall, nearly as tall as he was.

"Look at this," he called to his wife, "that will do the trick,", and he chuckled as he stuck a large pheasant's tail feather in the scarecrow's top hat.

"I just know this will frighten away those wretched rooks. They can go and hunt for food somewhere else from now on," he said with glee, rubbing his hands together.

"If it doesn't work," he said to his wife, "I'll eat his hat!" Not that he had any intention of doing that.

And so the potato field and Rose Cottage farm would come to have the pleasure of Mr Grundy's scarecrow doing its important job every spring when the rooks did most of the damage to the young potatoes. Although it was also the time of the year that the rooks were also feeding their newly-hatched chicks, Mr Grundy felt that this should be a problem for the adult rooks and he was happy to let them find their food elsewhere.

As they admired his work, Mrs Grundy turned to her husband and casually asked him, "What shall we call this magnificent scarecrow of yours? He must have a name; all scarecrows have names and identities."

"Hadn't thought about a name," he said as he tightened the binder twine around the scarecrow's middle, just tight enough to stop the straw from falling out of the front of the buttoned up raincoat. "Does he need one? Can't I just call him scarecrow?"

"Everyone needs a name, my dear, especially important people like this with a very important job to do," she replied with a quiet chuckle, "and I have the very name for it. We will call him Mr Fudge, because I think he has a sweet face, even if it is a turnip, and I like eating fudge."

"That's a silly name," retorted Mr Grundy, wrinkling his eyes into a frown. But he couldn't think of a better name, so to this very day their scarecrow who wears a long brown raincoat, black top hat with a pheasant's tail feather stuck in it, and a red scarf has been called Mr Fudge.

He should have lived quietly in the potato field by the corner gate, in summer and winter, in sun or rain. However, our tale doesn't end there; in fact, it's just the beginning. Strange events would take place on and around the farm and fields; some of them even involving Mr Fudge.

Once you get to know him you will realise what a remarkable scarecrow he is. He's not like others that you might see standing as a solitary sentinel in fields up and down the country. When it comes to scaring the rooks, there is no one better than Mr Fudge. The black birds with their huge grey bills and piercing eyes soon understood that he was not a person to cross. He stood five feet high, the tallest scarecrow in this part of Dorset, and when he spoke in 'scarecrow speak', the rooks would fly up in a flurry of feathers and squawks to hunt for grubs in the neighbouring fields.

Of course humans don't understand 'scarecrow speak', nor his funny ways. However, to their amazement and joy, both Lucy and William would come to learn how to communicate with Mr Fudge and with all his wildlife friends who lived near his potato field.

For his part, in return for their friendship, he introduced them to the ways and customs of the countryside and farms up and down the land. He told them which flowers they could pick and those that must not be touched because they were rare and very special and had to be kept safe for future generations.

A scarecrow's life can be a very happy one. There is always a lot going on around them and Mr Fudge was lucky that his raincoat had large deep pockets that soon provided an ideal home for a family of dormice. Every morning, in return for providing a cosy home, they would scamper all over him, tidying up any bits and pieces of loose straw that might annoy him during the day. He was particularly concerned about his red spotted neck scarf. If it was tidy and clean, then he felt the rest of him would be acceptable to his friends and to the children, so the dormice gave special attention to that piece of clothing.

On the other hand, what did annoy him were the uninvited visits of field mice. They had absolutely no respect for him or his position as guardian of the potato crop. These creatures were destructive, frequently smelly, and only had one objective when visiting him and that was to steal his straw to build their own nests at the bottom of the gate post.

Luckily, a long-eared owl and his family had their home in a large hole situated half way up the trunk of the old beech tree which stood close to him in the potato field. They were newcomers to the farm, having taken up residence last year. Mr Fudge was very happy to see the owls hunting the field mice and they did a remarkably good job. In return he agreed to keep the foxes and other owl predators away from their nest in the beech tree.

Life in the fields was something like a mutual society, where everyone helped each other. They all agreed that the field mice had to be kept under control because they breed so quickly. And as for the rooks, that was always a job well done during the potato growing season.

Chapter 3

Rose Cottage Farm

For as long as anyone could remember, farmer Grundy and his charming wife had lived in their small thatched cottage. His great great grandfather had come to live in this part of the county as a small boy, and Mr Grundy eventually acquired the farm and the cottage. Sadly, the Grundys do not have children who might one day continue to farm the land, so the line of Grundys would eventually be broken. The thought saddened them as they got older, because there were no parish records that go back far enough in time.

The Grundys have never really bothered to find out, but there might have been many generations of the family living in this part of Dorset. It is difficult to trace their family history, although when they were both much younger, Mr Grundy and his wife looked in their local church cemetery but found only one or two head stones with the name 'Grundy' engraved on them. Most of the others were difficult to read, due to years of weather damage and moss growth.

It was this lack of information about their family roots that made Mr Grundy and his wife especially interested in William and Lucy's story about the cave and how they found the glass bottle and message, and of course the fleeting image of the beautiful mermaid guarding the wooden sea chest. It would eventually prove to be a great stroke of luck that the children and their families had visited the farm, so many months ago. A lot had happened since that first meeting: accidents, surprises, great joy enjoyed by their friends, and events that would change their lives for ever. But before we can join them on these unexpected adventures we must know a little more about their cottage because its history is an important part of this adventure story.

Rose Cottage was built over four hundred years ago from local, rough cut limestone. A historian from the museum told them that in those days it was likely that the building stone came from a nearby quarry, because in this part of Dorset the underlying rock is limestone, famous for underground caverns.

When the villages were built, most of these old quarries had fallen into decay because there was no longer a need for the local stone. A few derelict ones can still be found, overgrown and sometimes full of deep, green, brackish water; certainly not the place to get lost in but wonderful places for bird watching and insect collecting.

In this part of the country it was also the custom for the owners to paint their cottages with white lime wash, just like Rose Cottage. Like many others in this part of the country, the cottage has two large wooden widows, each with four panes of glass. In between the two windows is a stout oak door with a large, weather-worn, black knocker.

Each summer a profusion of red and yellow climbing roses grows around the heavy oak door. They are Mrs Grundy's pride and joy. She tends them, talks to them, prunes them, ties them up when they get out of hand, and generally treats them as if they were her children. In return they repay her handsomely with an abundance of huge blooms.

Rose Cottage looks out onto the stream and the Roman bridge. The house has a single large brick chimney, surmounted by a dull red chimney pot that emits greyish smoke, summer and winter, whatever the weather. The smoke, which can be seen from all the fields on the farm, comes from an old Aga cooker in the kitchen. It burns wood, which is plentiful around the farm. By carefully controlling the dials Mr Grundy provides loads of hot water everyday and heat for his wife when she cooks.

Cooking is one of Mrs Grundy's passions. She bakes beautiful white bread every day and cakes – gorgeous cakes of all shapes and sizes, filled with delicious jam made from local berries that she picks from the hedgerows in the summer. Sometimes she thinks that the birds get the pick of the berry crop, and she mentions it to her husband, "Just a feeling," she said, "nothing definite, just a feeling, call it a woman's intuition."

Like most farms, the kitchen is where they spend most of their time when not out working on the farm or pottering around the yard. It's the largest room in the cottage, always cosy, with two old but very comfortable chairs either side of the Aga. The kitchen table has seen many years service. It is made of oak, with four chubby legs and is far too heavy to move but that doesn't matter because they never have to move it; there is plenty of space to walk around it without bumping into the Aga.

Against three of the kitchen walls stand majestic wooden, glass fronted dressers that reach to the beamed ceiling. They are full of china that has been collected over the years and tins of cooking ingredients. In its many drawers are stored the Grundy's cutlery and an amazing assortment of bits and pieces that 'might just be handy'.

In the corner opposite the back door, screwed into one of the black ceiling beams are three stout steel butchers' hooks. From these hang delicious joints of air-cured ham and bacon, ready to slice for breakfast or tea or whenever the fancy takes you, if you feel hungry for something special.

In the remaining part of the cottage is a smallish sitting room with two large windows that look out towards the bridge. They are kept shut to keep the flies out, especially during late summer. Behind the lounge is a bedroom with a low ceiling and wooden beams, just big enough to take a double bed, a wardrobe and two ancient Windsor chairs.

Next to the bedroom there is a newly built bathroom. It was added when the holiday home across the yard was built. Mrs Grundy well remembers the days when they were first married and she came to live at Rose Cottage. There was no bathroom then, nor the luxury of relaxing in a modern bath. If you wanted to relax after a hard sweaty day's work, you had to use a large copper tub in the kitchen, in front of the Aga. The tub was filled by a jug with hot steamy water. There was no need to worry about privacy in the kitchen in those days because no one ever came to visit.

Compared with other farms in the area, the Grundys' family farm is quite small, about two hundred acres. It is hidden in the folds of a valley, sitting on the side of a gently sloping, south facing hill, overlooked by clumps of trees. There are miles of unkempt hedges surrounding most of the grass fields.

To the north west and about half a mile from the farm there is a lake and a river that eventually flows into the harbour at Lyme Regis. The lake is popular with weekend dingy sailors who keep their boats moored on the western shore. Like other lakes in Dorset the shallow, gently sloping shore line is surrounded by water meadows. These are used by local farmers for grazing beef cattle and fattening sheep in the summer months, when the grass is lush. During the season the occasional fisherman can be seen huddled by the side of the lake, quietly waiting for a bite. Those who know the waters might be in luck because the lake teems with brown trout; but for those who don't, then it's the long trek back to the road and home, empty handed.

You wouldn't really call Mr Grundy a fisherman, but there is nothing he likes better than when his wife cooks him two grilled trout for his supper, done in butter and breadcrumbs. But you must never ask him where they came from nor how he acquired them. That would never do!

The lake is well known by nature lovers and locals for its variety of wildlife. Amongst the reeds along the water's edge are warblers and herons, and the swans can often be seen enjoying the freedom and solitude, rarely disturbed by man. On warm summer days when there is a gentle wind to russle the reed heads, a pair of buzzards fly in from the north to rise on the thermals high above the lake.

The lake is fed by the river that runs past Rose Cottage. It meanders past a large grass covered mound, close to the right hand bank, then alongside a ruined, roofless water mill and its clogged up water race, eventually to rush over shallow rapids between high overgrown banks before reaching the lake.

Rose Cottage farm has few farm buildings, unlike those on larger farms in the Midlands, which seem to be little villages. At Rose Cottage there is one Dutch barn for general use and, next to it, a number of round unthrashed wheat stacks that provide

Reed Warbler

grain for Mrs Grundy's hens and straw for other uses. There is an old tin shed that houses an ancient but precious tractor, and over the fence to the left is a large wooden hen house that stands off the ground on four wheels. Here live Mrs Grundy's Rhode Island Red chickens that enjoy a life of ease and luxury, except that is, when being bothered by the local vixen. Their large brown eggs, many of them 'double-yokers', keep the couple well provided throughout the year and are the reason why Mrs Grundy's cakes win so many prizes at local shows .

A few years ago, at the time that he had the extension to the bungalow done, Mr Grundy decided to add a small rectangular building that they hoped to use as a holiday home, renting it out to visitors, so as to improve the farm income. The new building sits opposite the wheat stacks and next to the grass bank that separates the yard from the river. It has a dark grey, tiled roof and a single chimney stack. Inside, there are two small bedrooms, a toilet and a separate bathroom.

For one reason or another they never got around to using it as a summer holiday home; instead, it became a storage place for odd bits of furniture and other accumulated clutter. In the summer and autumn it was ideal for storing apples and other fruit in the cool dry rooms. One of the two bedrooms had been converted into a kitchen storeroom, with shelves for jars and bottles of homemade wine and a great many tins of goodies. On a table in one corner stands a large grey metal container in which Mr Grundy soaks his hams and sides of bacon, using his 'secret curing solution'.

During the wet autumn and winter months the buildings are usually surrounded by muddy tracks, leading north to Lower Meadow or south from the cottage to the old bridge. The track over the bridge is the only way out of the farm and is constantly used by Mr Grundy in his old truck and his tractor and trailer. The bridge is their lifeline to the outside world. Without it they would be cut off, as happened many years ago when, after days of continuous heavy rains falling on the moors inland, the river flooded badly, leaving them stranded in the farm for over a week. Luckily, Mrs Grundy's well-stocked store cupboard kept the wolf from the door, as the saying goes.

The Heron

The farm consists mainly of grassland with one or two ploughed fields between the grazing. Because there is little outside work on the farm during the winter months, Mr Grundy enjoys the occasional day's shooting as he inspects his fields, at the same time hunting for rabbits that do so much damage to the grass. But Mr Grundy only shoots for the pot. Rabbits and pheasants, which are plentiful, are his favourite game, especially the way his wife cooks them slowly in the Aga in a large brown pot full of vegetables and herbs picked from their garden.

Although he shoots the occasional pheasant for eating, Mr Grundy has quite a passion for bird watching. You might think that this would conflict with his shooting pleasure: not so. Pheasants in the countryside always breed better if their numbers are controlled, so the odd day's shooting didn't worry him at all. The cottage and farm support an abundance of wildlife. Common bluetits and robins are plentiful in the large garden area behind the cottage and blackbirds and song thrushes are frequent visitors.

Mr Grundy particularly enjoys watching a magnificent grey heron that has a fishing position by the old bridge. It might be about five years old by the look of its plumage and the way it stalks the still waters. Early in the mornings, as the sun rises and before it gets too hot, it can be seen resting by the bridge, standing on one leg and with its eyes half-closed and head hunched between its shoulders.

It stands so still that you would think it is sleeping, but no, it is a patient bird, motionless until a slight ripple in the water reveals an eel, a small fish, or even a frog. Then the bird summons a lightening reflex and in a flash his head pierces the water, reappearing with the victim in its beak. The bird's bill, like a pick-axe, is a lethal weapon, feared by small mammals as well as the fish. Such is nature in the wild and we must accept its harshness and not try to change it.

The heron will eat small fish head first in a couple of gulps. If he is lucky to catch a larger fish, he will stab it before taking it to the bank to eat. His manners leave a lot to be desired.

Of all the birds that live on or near the farm, Mr Grundy most dislikes the black rooks. They are very sociable birds, pairing for life and nesting in colonies that they return to each spring. They are also thieves and can often be seen stealing twigs from each other's nests when the rightful owners are away collecting nesting material. The nearest of these treetop rookeries, loud with hoarse cawing, is not far from Bluebell Wood in two old oak trees that form the boundary between Lower and Upper Meadows.

Mr Grundy's dislike for these birds is mainly due to the damage they do to his new potatoes when the delicate green shoots emerge from the soil a few weeks after planting. The birds go for anything that can be eaten and do not discriminate between these new shoots and the harmful grubs of the yellow wire worms, nor brown slugs. Now, thank goodness, with Mr Fudge standing guard over the potato crop the rooks had had to change their feeding habits and fly the few miles to neighbours' farms to hunt for their food.

As the early spring recedes and another year of crocuses and snowdrops dies off, to be replaced by daffodils, Mr and Mrs Grundy look forward to the arrival of the returning swallows. They are always welcome visitors to their farm, especially the two families of swallows that return early each summer from North Africa to the same nests they used the year before. One family raises their chicks in the Dutch barn, whilst the others occupy a good site under the roof of the tin shed, near to the door.

The swallows' distinctive saucer shaped nests are made from dried grass mixed with regurgitated mud collected from the tracks around the farm. When the tracks in the yard are dry, there is plenty of suitable mud at the base of the bridge, where it is churned up by the heron. Mr Grundy admires the way the swallows feed on

The Swallow

39

the wing, bombing and swooping to catch flying insects. Sometimes they will skim a few inches over the water near the bridge and catch a dragonfly.

William and Lucy love to watch the swallows when they spend their holidays with the Grundys on the farm. They visit when they can get away from home for a few weeks and there's no summer camp to attend. It was on one of their early visits that they met Mr Fudge and became such close friends. They clearly remembered the first time they saw the tall, scruffily dressed scarecrow. At first, they thought he was just another ordinary farm scarecrow who lived in a potato field. However, Lucy did think there was something unusual about him. She mentioned it to William when they went to bed that night.

"Is it his clothes, William?" she asked. "It scares me the way it looks at me with those large black eyes. I get a shiver up my spine. What do you think?"

She and William talked about it for a long time until they both crawled under their duvets and fell asleep, exhausted by another day's fun and activity on the farm.

After lunch the next day, without saying a word to Mr Grundy or his wife, the two retraced their steps across Lower Meadow to the potato field. Walking through the opened gate, they quietly approached the scarecrow. He stood motionless with both arms outstretched, just as they had seen him the day before. Of course, they didn't know it had been a busy morning for him, scaring away unwanted visitors, particularly the rooks from the rookery.

William and Lucy stood in front of the scarecrow, looking up at his long red nose and his crumpled top hat with its pheasant tail sticking out at a jaunty angle. Suddenly, to their amazement, a strong, clear, male voice spoke out, making them both jump back and nearly falling over each other.

"Good afternoon, and who might you two be?"

Lucy steadied herself as best she could and held her ground, mouth wide open, heart beating fast. The invisible voice spoke again.

"My name is Mr Fudge, what's yours?"

"Wow! exclaimed William, not believing what he had just heard. "Did you hear that Lucy"?

"I … I'm William," he blurted out, thinking it was rather foolish to be talking to what appeared to be a dummy, "and this is my sister Lucy."

Lucy closed her mouth, took a deep breath and turning round to her brother said, "Don't be silly William! How can it possibly speak, it doesn't have a proper mouth, and anyway, look, it only has a turnip head." She stared closely at the scarecrow, not wanting to believe what she had just heard.

"Less of the turnip head young lady,"replied the scarecrow. "I can talk, and what is more, I can think too, just like you. I can understand humans and right now I know what you both are thinking. Of course," he continued, "I can't move, but I am a very special scarecrow. I was made from a stout pole cut in Bluebell Wood. In that wood there are mystical powers that I have inherited and that is why I am able to speak to you".

"Golly gosh!" gasped Lucy, still shaking a little from the initial shock of hearing the scarecrow speak. "You can talk like us," she said, grabbing hold of William's arm for reassurance as she looked up into Mr Fudge's face. As she looked she now began to see more human-like features appearing where once she had seen only a turnip and a carrot nose. Indeed, the closer she studied his face, the more pronounced the features seemed to become.

"My name is Mr Fudge"

"Of course I can," he replied.

For a split second Lucy thought she saw a faint smile on his face and, for the first time during this extraordinary meeting, she started to relax slightly.

William plucked up courage and asked sheepishly, "Please Mr Scarecrow, what did you say your name was?"

"It's Mr Fudge," he answered briskly. "Mr Fudge to you young man and don't forget the Mister. Everybody knows me round here, especially those rooks from the rookery."

"Mr Fudge," repeated Lucy as she stood in front of him, wanting to shield William from whatever the scarecrow might do next. "Well Mr Fudge, you gave us both quite a fright. We were only expecting a dummy scarecrow, like the ones we have read about."

"A dummy, a dummy scarecrow!" cried out Mr Fudge, obviously hurt by her remark, and his straw-filled arms flapped slightly in the afternoon breeze. "Let me tell you both, there's not a finer scarecrow in all of Dorset."

"Oh I'm sure you're right Mr Fudge, we won't make that mistake again, will we William?" she said, giving him a nudge.

It was a difficult few minutes but soon the three of them began to chat together, almost like old friends, until Mr Fudge reminded them that it was their teatime and they better get back to the farm before Mr Grundy came looking for them. The children agreed, but before they left they promised to meet him the next day and they apologised for thinking that he was just a dummy.

"Think nothing of it my friends," he replied, "but please don't say a word to anyone. We mustn't frighten the old folk, must we? Do you promise?" They promised him.

Over the next few days they made secret visits to the potato field and got to know Mr Fudge better. They quickly mastered his way of talking and he managed to understand Lucy, despite her habit of speaking too fast. William was a little more reticent and said very little at first, but his shyness was soon overcome when Mr Fudge realised how interested William was in nature. William found black beetles and other insects at the base of Mr Fudge's pole and showed them to him. They soon knew that they had a lot in common with each other and over the days and weeks that followed, the scarecrow introduced William and Lucy to his friends who lived in the woods and hedgerows.

The children told Mr Fudge about the way humans lived … well, the way they lived at home with their Mummy and Daddy, two guinea pigs and the goldfish. They mentioned Grandma Ruthie's cats, but soon realised that cats who are uncontrollable were not welcomed in the fields, or by Mr Fudge, so they never mentioned them again.

Farms like this one in Dorset, with its grass fields and overgrown hedges, attract large families of rabbits. They live everywhere, in burrows hidden in the undergrowth of hedges and, on the Grundys' farm, in at least two locations near Bluebell Wood, where the warrens were like small towns. No wonder Mr Grundy shoots them occasionally; it's the only way to keep their numbers down. Surprisingly, even Mr Fudge accepted this, although deep down he didn't really approve of shooting wild creatures.

Families of mice colonise every spare hiding place amongst the farm buildings, under the hen house and wheat stacks. They are everywhere and when Lucy and William walk very slowly without making a sound, they can see the furry little creatures playing amongst the sacks in the Dutch barn. Of course where there are mice there will be owls and these two barn owls took up residence a number of years ago in the old shed. Here they hatch a family each year. Over in Bluebell Wood, Mr Fudge told the

The Barn Owls

children that a pair of long-eared owls had lived there over the last few years.

"You'll only see them at night when they come out to hunt for food," he advised them.

Mr Fudge had names for all these creatures, friend and foe alike. He was never happier than when introducing them to Lucy and William. However, he kept the biggest surprise of all until late one special afternoon.

In the early evenings at the end of most days, just before tea, Lucy and William would walk across Lower Meadow to the potato field to chat to Mr Fudge. On this particular warm summer evening they noticed that Mr Fudge was in a good mood, which pleased Lucy, although it never bothered William one way or the other.

"Have you had a good day scaring the rooks?" she asked as they sat down on the dry grass by his side.

"I have," he said, looking down at them with a slight smile on his turnip face.

Before they had time to tell him about their day, he coughed, cleared his throat –well, that's what it sounded like – and asked them, "Have you seen the Little People that live in Bluebell Wood?"

"Pardon?" they both said together. "Who are they?"

"I will have to introduce them to you," he said in an authoritative voice, "but first you will have to meet my very dear friend Benjamin when he comes to visit me, which I hope will be quite soon. Benjamin lives in a house under a big pile of tree trunks and logs behind the Dutch barn at Rose Cottage."

"Is he another scarecrow, this Benjamin person?" Lucy asked.

"Does Mr Grundy know he lives there?" chipped in William, suddenly finding his voice.

"I'm sure he doesn't, William. You must both understand that Benjamin is a bit like me. He's spent all his life in the countryside but has only recently taken up residence at Rose Cottage farm."

"Why Rose Cottage farm?" asked William.

There was no reply to his question and Mr Fudge continued, "He knows where the Little People live. I can't walk because I only have one leg and I'm always stuck in this ground," said Mr Fudge showing some frustration in his voice. "So, I will have to ask him to take you to introduce you to their tribe."

"Who are these Little People that live in a tribe?" William asked for the second time.

"Young man, wait until you meet Benjamin then he'll tell you all about them," said Mr Fudge. An owl hooted loudly somewhere in the wood and another joined in on the other side of the potato field as if replying to the first call.

"It's time for their supper and it's time you two walked back to the farm before it gets too dark and the Grundys wonder what you have been up to."

With this exciting news ringing in their ears, the two slowly made their way back to the farm. They were tired, but not tired enough to stop talking all the way back about Benjamin.

"I wonder what he might look like, how old he is, and who are these Little People?" said Lucy.

They also wondered just how small these Little People might be and what they might look like.

Chapter 4

The Little People

Two days after Mr Fudge's announcement about Benjamin, Lucy and William strolled purposefully across Lower Meadow, making their way towards the potato field. They were naturally both excited but had no idea what he was going to tell them this time.

Their minds were full of thoughts about Benjamin and the Little People. Where did they live, how many are there and would they all become friends? It had been the main topic of their secret conversations during the last two days.

Although he wasn't really sure, William had a feeling that Mrs Grundy knew something was up. She hadn't said anything but on more than one occasion she had given him that funny look, as if to say, what are you two up to? But, thank goodness, she never asked, otherwise William wouldn't have known what to say. He couldn't lie but on the other hand, he didn't want to tell the truth just yet.

This afternoon the rooks were particularly active and noisy. They rarely visited the potato field now for fear of Mr Fudge, and as the two children walked past the rookery with its pungent damp smell, they spotted the lookouts whose job it was to warn the rest of the flock if trouble was about. A few of the adult birds became excited and as the children approached, the whole black flock rose up squawking and calling to each other, dancing in the sky until the danger was passed and they could settle back down onto their perches and nests.

Lucy and William ignored the flock of birds and made their way across the grass towards the potato field to see Mr Fudge, comfortable in the thought that, thanks to his teaching, they now they knew more about how rooks react. As they neared the gate leading into the field, Lucy pointed out a figure to William, walking towards them down the hedge.

"William," she whispered, "I think it's that Benjamin person coming towards us." Although they had not seen him before, they recognised him at once from Mr Fudge's description. The clothes he wore were very distinctive, especially his hat and hunting-type jacket and heavy farm boots.

"Good morning you two," he called out, and they greeted each other with a friendly smile and wave as if they had known each other for years. "I'm Benjamin, and you must be William, and if I'm not mistaken, this must be your pretty sister, Lucy. Pleased to meet you both. Mr Fudge has told me all about you and has asked me to introduce you to the Little People.

"I have known the tribe of Little People for many many years, in fact at least a hundred," he said without

"Good morning you two, my name's Benjamin"

blinking an eyelid. "For a number of reasons, you'll find that they are uneasy in the company of humans."

Lucy looked at William and mouthed so quietly that Benjamin couldn't hear her, "A hundred years, did you hear that?"

"However," Benjamin continued, unaware of their reaction, "I've had a word with their Leader and although he is a little cautious, Mr Fudge has said such nice things about you that he is happy for you to meet the Little People in their home."

As they continued their walk together towards the potato field he started to tell them all about Bluebell Wood. He pointed towards the other end of the field, where tall trees waving their branches stood amongst the smaller trees, whose branches and leaves hung down and touched the ground, making lovely hiding places.

"Is that Bluebell Wood?" William asked excitedly. "That's the wood that Mr Grundy was telling us about Lucy," he said, turning to his sister.

"Benjamin, are there bluebells there in the spring?"she asked. "And are there strange noises, because Mr Grundy doesn't like going into the wood, but has never told us why."

"Well," answered Benjamin, pausing before continuing. "Sometimes there is an eerie whistling sound as if the trees are alive and talking to each other. And then there are other times when the whole wood is still and silent like the grave and nothing stirs. But Lucy, please don't worry. I will be taking both of you to the wood because that's where the Little People live. If you believe you will be safe, then you will be safe. There is nothing in the wood to hurt you or scare you, trust me."

Goose pimples ran up and down Lucy's arms as Benjamin continued his story and she thought about the wood. She felt excited but also a tiny bit afraid. She had never in her whole life ever been to the centre of a mysterious wood before, not even with her father. This was going to be a new experience and both she and William thought it was a bit spooky, to say the least. However, as long as she was with her brother, and Benjamin was telling them the truth, she knew she would be safe.

By now they were nearly at the gate leading into the potato field. There was Mr Fudge, standing majestically, arms out-stretched, enjoying what he likes doing most, standing guard.

"I see you've met our two friends, Benjamin?" he said. "Have you told them about our other good friends, the Little People who live in Bluebell Wood?"

"Yes I have, but only some of the story. I can finish it on the way to the clearing," said Benjamin confidently.

"Good, that's very good," said Mr Fudge, in that very authoritative voice of his which the children had now got quite use to hearing.

"William, can I just say to you and your sister, that Benjamin is a very old friend of mine. Like me, he is wise about the ways of the countryside, but unlike me he can't talk the languages

Bluebell Wood

of the wild creatures, which is a pity but can't be helped. However, he is very close to the Little People, so please do exactly as he asks you all times."

His words left a strong impression in the minds of the two children as the four of them chatted some more, before being interrupted by Benjamin.

"Let's go then," he said and smiled at Fudge. Turning, he beckoned to Lucy and William to follow him out of the potato field. They turned left through the gate and walked briskly towards Upper Meadow, while Benjamin took up the story once again.

"In the middle of the wood that we're walking towards is a large clearing," he explained. "It's overgrown with grass and wild flowers in the summer. At other times of the year you have to be careful of brambles and white nettles, they're everywhere," he told them.

"In the centre of the clearing there is a tall, twisted, ancient tree stump covered in ivy and moss. It is the remains of an ancient oak, that I believe thrived when King Arthur and his warriors roamed this land. Some think the stump has mystical powers and that's why humans keep well away from this part of the wood. It won't be too long before you two know the real truth."

The Stump in the woodland clearing

By now they had walked half way up Upper Meadow and were approaching the dark edge of the wood. Lucy tentatively put out her hand to grab William's for reassurance and felt a slight tremor in his. She didn't say a word because there was no way she wanted to give the impression to Benjamin that she was scared, even though she was shaking a little.

Benjamin spoke, breaking the silence, and it immediately helped Lucy to overcome her fears. "When we get to the clearing please walk carefully across the grass to the stump without making too much noise; in fact, don't talk. When you get to it, if you bend down and look hard at its base, hidden under long twisting roots and the overhanging moss, you'll see a hole like a badger's hole, just big enough for a person to crawl in to. It's too small for big adults though."

He beckoned to the children to follow him towards a gap in the hedge a few yards in front of them. "When we get to the stump, look inside the hole and you'll see there's a door. Beyond this door is a short flight of stone steps that leads deep down into the ground."

"Where do the steps lead to, Benjamin?" asked Lucy, now showing more confidence than she had done a few moments ago.

"You'll soon find out," he answered in a quiet comforting voice. "Just wait and see."

"Look over here; see this gap in the hawthorn hedge, just here? It's been made by the local badger family for as long as I can remember and it's the easiest way for them to get from this field to the wood the other side where they live. We can only get through it one at a time."

They took it in turns to push their way through the low gap, finding themselves on the other side of the hedge and up to their waists in long grass. They were surrounded by thick dense bushes and trees. The ground was covered in nettles and brambles as far as the eye could see.

How are we going to push our way through this lot, thought William as he scratched his leg on the thorns of a bramble.

"Over here," shouted Benjamin, just off to their left. Struggling through the long grass that tugged at their legs they managed to get to him, although Lucy wasn't too happy about things. She hated nettles, but had cleverly negotiated the route without getting stung.

For the first time, William noticed the silence around them. It was perfectly still and the trees were quiet, with no breeze passing through their branches to disturb them. To his surprise there was no bird song, which he would have expected in this woodland. He glanced up into the highest branches of the elm tree above them, hoping to see a rook's nest or maybe one left behind by some pigeons: but nothing. He shuddered and goose pimples appeared on his arms and he didn't know why.

Everywhere was eerie and still. Lucy was momentarily lost in thought as she looked around. The place reminded her of the Bambi video they had back at home, but this was more sinister and she shivered, even though it was warm in the dappled shade of the trees.

"Come on you two, we mustn't waste time dawdling." Benjamin had found the path he was looking for and started to lead them down the twisting route. It was just wide enough to allow them to walk down in single file without being snared by the brambles. The tall nettles and brambles created a sort of narrow woodland street, so

dense that it stopped them from straying away from the path. It seemed to the children that the undergrowth was guarding something very special from their gaze.

Benjamin obviously knew the path like the back of his hand. They had been following him for about fifteen minutes, when he called out, just loud enough for them to hear, "We're here."

They stepped out of the semi-darkness of the wood and stood at the edge of the clearing that Benjamin had told them about earlier. There, right in front of them, just as he had described it, stood the old stump, covered in dark green moss and brown twisting roots. It looked like a ruined cathedral, lit by shafts of sunlight that shone through the clearing. The children were spellbound in wonder at their discovery.

Benjamin watched Lucy and William as they walked slowly towards the stump. They stopped and turned round to him for guidance. He nodded as if to say, "Look for the hole".

"I can't see the hole," said Lucy.

"Nor can I," said William, examining the wide base of the old oak tree.

"If you walk round to the other side, you will," said Benjamin.

They did as he told them and there it was, half hidden by moss and a tangle of overhanging roots. The two were so excited they stood with their mouths open, not believing their eyes. Was this true or were they both dreaming?

Lucy whispered to William so quietly that he could hardly hear her, "William, it's like Alice in Wonderland. You know, that bit when she falls asleep under the tree and finds the hole."

"That was a fairy tale," he whispered back. "This is real, Lucy, it's really happening to us, isn't it?"

"Shall we open the door and go down?" asked William, plucking up courage. He thought he might just be able to crawl through the hole if he kept his head down.

"In a minute," said Benjamin who had joined them. "First, I must make sure that the Little People really want to see us today."

"How will you know if they want to?" asked Lucy excitedly.

"Well," said Benjamin thoughtfully, "if they didn't want to see us, we wouldn't be able to see the entrance at the base of this stump. Somehow, and I don't know how, they would manage to hide it from us."

"But I can see the hole in the stump," said Lucy, "and look, it has a small door in it, just as you described it to us. Does that mean they want to meet us? Are there really small people living underground, Benjamin, through that door and down those steps?" She had a hint of reservation in her voice, thinking to herself, what they would look like, how will we talk to them, would they like us? Questions whizzed around her head, but nothing came out of her mouth.

"Yes. I can tell you that they are happy to meet us. So, I'll go first. Lucy, you follow behind me and William, will you close the door behind you please?"

The three friends crouched down on bended knees ready to crawl through the hole, but before they moved forward an inch it suddenly became much larger. In fact it became big enough to make it quite easy to stand upright and walk through the door. They climbed down a short flight of rickety stone steps that led into a huge underground cavern. At the foot of the steps Benjamin stopped and looked around as if he expected to see someone, but the cavern was deserted and eerily silent. The earth and rock walls were covered with hanging tree roots of all sizes and the floor felt brick-hard under their feet. William thought that the roof, high above their heads, was made of rock, but he wasn't sure.

When Benjamin told them about the cavern they imagined it be be a dark, dank, smelly cave, but this huge cavern was a magical sight, lit by thousands of twinkling lights that were suspended from the roof and walls. The children were enthralled by the soft yellow light that bathed everything it touched.

William, being a rather inquisitive person, always wanting to know how things work, walked towards the nearest clutch of twinkling lights. "Look at these Lucy," he said in awe, pointing to a group of the lights hanging just above his head. "I don't believe it. Look, all these lights are tiny insects. I wonder if they're glow worms?"

Benjamin stood with his two new friends and shared their delight at the scene. He had been there many times before but he was still fascinated by the sight.

As they stood in the silence of the cavern, their attention was drawn to a slight movement at the far end. Out of the semi-darkness a strange creature moved towards them. It was over five feet tall and covered in hair, and it was followed by other, slightly smaller creatures, until there were so many standing in front of Lucy that she couldn't count them.

William froze, his mouth open in amazement and his eyes as round as saucers. Lucy edged slowly behind Benjamin for comfort as she stared at the creature that approached them with his hand stretched out. The soft light picked out human-like features and Lucy wondered just what sort of creature it might be.

Benjamin walked forward towards the figure and took hold of the outstretched hairy hand. "Hello Leader," he said. "These are the young human friends we told you about. This one is Lucy and this is her brother William. They are staying at Rose Cottage farm."

The Leader moved towards them. "Welcome to our home," he said in a very strange, low and gravely voice.

William murmured to Lucy, "He can speak nearly the way we do Lucy. He must be human like us, but why doesn't he look like us?"

He turned to Benjamin, "Why are they so hairy?" he asked.

"Not now William, I'll tell you later, on the way home."

Turning back to the Leader, Benjamin continued, "Leader, we are here so that you can meet my two friends and they can meet you and the rest of your tribe. Our very good friend Mr Fudge has promised William and Lucy that he would teach them all the wonders of the countryside, the secrets and habits of the wildlife and the beauty of all the plants that you and I take so much for granted.

"He wants you to help, please, and I believe he knows they will repay this kindness, over time and in their own way. He hasn't discussed what that might be with me, but as you know Leader, he has the ability to look into the future for all of us."

The Leader stepped forward and with great presence took William and Lucy by the arm and led them to a low rock shelf that ran along the length of the cavern.

"Sit down here," he commanded, politely but firmly. "Would you like something to eat?" He swept the hair from his face so that they could see him more clearly. He had a kind face with dark brown eyes, deep set below bushy eyebrows.

"Yes please," said William, because he was always hungry.

Suddenly the cavern erupted in excited chatter as the Little People rushed about to find fruit, nuts and juicy vegetables, which they served to their guests on green plates, woven from the fibres of huge leaves.

Although everyone seemed very happy, Lucy noticed that there wasn't too much closeness. The younger ones kept their distance and it was only the Leader who came to sit with them.

Benjamin was very careful not to overstay their welcome. It was their first visit and he was delighted at how well it had gone. By the look on their faces the children had enjoyed themselves and it seemed that the Leader had indicated their acceptance by his tribe. That was important.

Sometime later Benjamin led the children back to Mr Fudge's farm gate and they said "Good Night" to their new friend. Benjamin would tell Mr Fudge how successful their first meeting had been.

Lucy and William got back to the cottage just before tea. Mrs Grundy asked them what they had been doing during the afternoon and they had to be careful about what they said. Benjamin had warned them both to say nothing about their exploits in Bluebell Wood.

"If you tell the grown-ups what has happened to us today they might laugh at us, so just say you have been learning about the countryside with some new friends and leave it at that."

That's what Lucy and William said, which of course was the truth, but not quite the whole truth.

That summer holiday was full of long warm, balmy, days. When Lucy and William could get away from the grown-ups they spent many hours talking to Mr Fudge about farming and countryside myths and traditions.

The potato crop was growing well and the rooks behaved, keeping away most of the time. When Mr Fudge took a snooze, a bird would occasionally fly down from the rookery to grab a small potato poking through the soil. But this wasn't a serious problem, as potatoes that find themselves uncovered by soil normally turn green and then they're no good for harvesting, but excellent for rooks.

During the next four weeks, whenever they could, they visited the clearing in the wood. They checked that the door was there, then climbed down the rickety stone steps to spend many happy hours with the Little People, learning all about their strange customs and ways. In return, William and Lucy told them the things that humans in the outside world do.

The Leader and William developed a strong bond between them, spending a lot of time in each other's company, talking about the tribe's history. The tribe had no books, nor could they write letters or words to communicate to each other. It was all spoken history, handed down from one generation to the next.

It was during these periods that William began to realise that although the Little People couldn't write like humans, they had remarkable skills in many other ways. For instance, they could see in the dark and they could talk to each other without making any sound. It was a trick that William wanted to learn, because it would be fun to try it at school with Lucy. But what really fascinated him was their ability to memorise the very smallest details, especially about events that happened so many years ago.

One night, as they were getting ready for bed, William turned to Lucy and said, "Lucy, I've been thinking. Do you think the Little People are really human beings? They're not like you and me, or even the Grundys, but they have so many human characteristics. In some things they're better than us, like being able to see in the dark."

Lucy sat on the edge of her bunk bed and took her diary out from under her pillow as she pondered William's question. "If they're human beings, William, why do they live underground, and why are they covered in so much hair all over their bodies?"

Deep down, what he had said made her think about their experiences over the last few weeks in the cavern. She had been surprised at how quickly the younger ones had grasped the things she had shown them. Already they could nearly speak like her and they walked upright like she did, even though they looked hunched up and slightly round shouldered. And when they laughed, their faces looked human, even under all that untidy hair. Like us, she thought, but somehow strangely different. Their carefree days on the farm flew past and soon it was time to pack their cases once again for the journey home to Warwickshire. Daddy would come to fetch them if he wasn't flying and they hoped that Mummy would come too, if she wasn't working. The plan was to have lunch together with the Grundys, then to leave early in the afternoon. It would be late by the time they got home.

"Why do the holidays have to end so soon?" moaned William as he helped Lucy to tidy their room. Mrs Grundy always insisted they tidied the room, even on their last day at the farm.

"You have to go back to school William,".she answered, 'Have you forgotten you are going up to the senior school next term?"

"Oh yes," he said with slight excitement in his voice. He had forgotten, but now he felt much better about leaving Rose Cottage and his friends. Anyway, they'd soon be back, he thought, as he sat on his case and asked his big sister to close the locks for him, which she did with ease.

They still hadn't told anyone about their adventures in Bluebell Wood. William knew that they could not break their promise to Mr Fudge and Benjamin, that they would not reveal their secret 'until the time is right'. Even if he did tell his parents, he reasoned, would they believe the stories about Bluebell Wood and the stump, the cavern, and their happy times with the Little People?

Maybe it would be too much for adults to understand, he decided, and he vowed not to tell a soul, not even his best friend Charlie at school.

Chapter 5

Fun with the Little People

The autumn term had been hard work with loads of homework and plenty of sport to keep their minds and bodies fully occupied. How quickly holidays arrived and they found themselves once more on the farm in Dorset for half term. It was one of those 'helping Mr Grundy' days. William was wearing the oldest, dirtiest clothes he could find, much to Mrs Grundy's annoyance as she always liked him to look smart, even on the farm.

He was in his element in the Dutch barn, moving bits of machinery around. He tidied this and packed away that and, with the largest broom he could find, made clouds of dust as he swept the hard earth floor, pushing a large pile of rubbish towards the door. It wasn't his favourite job, but anything to help Mr Grundy is a bonus, he thought to himself, you never know when you might need a favour in return. This was very astute, as favours are like having money in the bank, available if you need it.

This morning, Lucy was on her own for once. When William announced he was going to help clean out the barn, she decided to do her own 'typical girl' thing! Cleaning dirty farm buildings and getting herself covered in dust from head to toe was not a job for a girl; well, not this girl anyway!

Half term gave them only one week off from school work, and they particularly wanted to meet the Little People again in their cavern. It was much more exciting here at Rose Cottage than back home, even though there were school friends for sleep-overs and other things to do. But it was such fun to be on the farm, spending time with extraordinary characters and doing things they couldn't do at home.

It was autumn and the weather had changed to cooler days and colder nights. The swallows had left for warmer countries, flying thousands of miles to Africa. They would return to the same nests next spring to bring up another brood of chicks. In the rookery on the north side of Lower Meadow, the youngsters had grown into young adults and many had flown off to establish another rookery. It would be close to their birth place but just far enough away so that they wouldn't annoy their parents. The cocky sparrows were still hanging around the cottage and farm buildings, along with the robins and their broods who had made permanent homes in the shrubs at the end of the vegetable garden.

Two birds they expected to see were missing, the two barn owls that were Lucy's favourites. She was worried that during the summer an accident had befallen them. She knew that if one was left on its own, it would fly to another site. That would be so sad. She would ask Mr Fudge about them. He knows everything there is to know about what's going on around the farm, she thought, and is certainly the best person to ask about the owls.

The Robin

There wasn't any cooking that Lucy could help Mrs Grundy with, which was a shame because she loved to get her hands covered in flour. Mrs Grundy had prepared as much food as possible in advance so that she could spend more time with the children. If only she had known that cooking was one of Lucy's great pleasures, she would have left some to do together. Perhaps some of her sponge cakes, which were famous as the best at school and a great favourite with Papo.

"I'm going out for a walk," she told Mrs Grundy who was washing some particularly dirty clothes in the large white sink by the back door.

"I might just go along Lower Meadow and take a look at the scarecrow," she said as she put on her coat, wrapping a long warm woolly scarf around her neck in case it turned cold out in the fields. At this time of the year in the South West, the weather can change suddenly and the last thing she wanted today was to get wet or cold.

Stepping out of the back door and closing it behind her, she turned left in front of the wheat stacks, walked through the yard gate and closed it behind her. As she walked past the wooden hen house a few chickens clucked and moved out of her way.

The noise and commotion coming from the Dutch barn told her that William was hard at work doing his cleaning chores. If she called out to him she thought he would want to know where she was going, but this morning she had decided that by telling Mrs Grundy a little white lie, and not telling William, she could visit the cavern without anyone knowing. It wasn't in her nature to be dishonest; it was really a case of not mentioning the real reason for going out for a walk.

Although today would be the first time on her very own, she had been to the stump several times before and was no longer afraid of the wood or the secrets it held. As she trudged across the grass, damp after last night's heavy dew, towards the badger gap in the boundary hedge, she felt slightly apprehensive and goose bumps appeared up and down her arms.

She wriggled through the gap in the hedge and found the path on the other side. The brambles had been stripped clean of their fruit, either by the birds, thought Lucy, or by the Little People who lived on fruit and other wild food.

Lucy sensed the magic of the woodland in autumn. The leaves were changing colour from dark green to beautiful oranges, browns and yellows, and some had started to fall, covering the floor with a carpet of exquisite colours. The path was still passable, although the brambles and nettles tried their hardest to cover it in places. Grasses were turning winter brown and were

falling in all directions, creating hidden runways for mammals to scamper through from one safe haven to the next. As she made her way to the clearing, Lucy wondered if the owls were in the wood.

She went past the last of the beech trees guarding the clearing towards the old stump, looking a little bedraggled at the end of the summer, but still with its mystic charm. It was surrounded by brambles and in places she could see that the drab fungi had been chewed by mice.

She felt a little less nervous now that she had reached the stump and she found the door where she expected it to be. It only needed a slight push and it opened to reveal the steps down into the cavern. Stooping down, she walked down the steps to the cavern. As she expected, everywhere was bathed in that soft yellow light, throwing faint shadows on the walls and ceiling.

She felt excited, it was obvious that the Little People were expecting her, but how did they know she was coming to visit them? She had no idea, except that the door at the top of the steps was there, and that if she hadn't found it, she could not have entered their home. They must have a sixth sense about me coming, she thought, or perhaps they were warned by some of their friends when I first entered the wood.

There was frantic activity as the Little People crowded around her, touching her dress. Several tried to grab her hands to pull her towards one of the cavern shelves, eager to show her things they had collected. Their happy jabbering showed how pleased were they to see her without Benjamin or William getting in the way; something that boys are very good at doing.

Earlier that morning while eating breakfast, she had made up her mind to visit the Little People because there were some questions that she needed answering. Lucy hated it when there were questions unanswered, especially about these strange but lovable hairy creatures that lived underground, that didn't really look like her but could speak like her.

She was determined to find out more. It was her mummy who had said to her a few months before, "Lucy, if you want to find out more about anything, then you must ask. If it involves other people then you must face them and politely ask the right questions." She remembered that now, as she found herself surrounded in this strange place by the group of Little People.

Turning to the one that she thought was the oldest, she asked, "Why are you so friendly with Mr Fudge and how long have you known him?" Then lots of other questions came tumbling out before the creature had time to answer the first one.

"Well Lucy, ever since Farmer Grundy made Mr Fudge a few years ago," he said, and they all started to laugh and chatter amongst themselves as if it was a big joke.

"I'll let you into one of our special secrets," he managed to say once the chattering had quietened down. "Did you know that our scarecrow friend Mr Fudge is made from a stout pole cut from one of our sacred trees that grows here in Bluebell Wood? We don't think Mr Grundy knew that at the time he cut the pole, it just happened that way, it was a coincidence," he said, smiling to her under his mass of hair. She couldn't see the smile but knew by the tone of his voice that he was smiling at her and that made her pleased and warm inside.

So that's why he is who he is, she thought to herself as she listened intently to the answers to all her other questions. Now that she knew the secret she would have to tell William, but maybe not the others, not yet anyway.

"Is this the reason why humans disliked coming to Bluebell Wood?" she asked more boldly, wondering what the answer might be. "Does it really have magical powers that only the Little People and others like Benjamin and Mr Fudge know about?"

As she listened intently to his answers she wondered if there were other supernatural powers which she had yet to find out about, such as where did the Little People originally come from? Why do they live underground and not above ground, and who are they, really? She began to feel nervous again.

"Lucy, I get the feeling that you seem to be worried about something I've said," the largest of the Little People murmured to her, sensing her unease. How did he know that, she thought as she started to tell him of her fears about Bluebell Wood, the unknown mystical powers that seemed to exist in this place, and about a scarecrow that is made from ordinary farm material but has an incredible ability to look into the future, to talk to her and William about so many things, and in their own language too.

"Please don't worry. In time you and William will come to understand all there is to know about us and our friends and about the true life in the countryside. Yes, there are ancient myths and legends that haunt our home here in the cavern, but you are not ready to share these yet. It will all be revealed to you when our Leader feels that the time is right."

Lucy listened, fascinated by these answers. There would be more, she thought. The feeling that she and William would eventually be let into the darkest history of the Little People filled her with excitement. But when would it happen? Soon, she hoped.

"Let me start now, Lucy, by telling you something which I hope will interest you. We have lived underground in this cavern for as long as we can remember. Our elders taught us to live with nature and to respect what it gives to us We are what we are and what you see before you. We are different to normal humans; we rarely venture into the outside world because our history, handed down by one leader to the next, tells us to be cautious of humans. What would they do to us if they caught us?" There was silence because she had no answer to that question.

"If we have to go out at night to collect berries, nuts and vegetables from Farmer Grundy's farm or other places, we need someone to look out

"Mr Fudge was made with a magic pole from Bluebell Wood"

for us and that's what Mr Fudge and all his feathered friends do. They warn us if humans are coming or if there is danger about," he told her.

"If humans get to close, we quickly make our way back to the clearing and the cavern. The humans believe our wood is haunted and they won't come into it. You see Lucy, they think it's full of magic and strange happenings, but it isn't really. We just make them think it is to keep them away."

"That's clever," she replied, "because William and I were scared the first time we visited you with Benjamin. Did you know that?"

"You asked us why we know Mr Fudge," he continued, not answering her question, but happier that Lucy was feeling more relaxed and comfortable in his company. Many of the other Little People had wandered off, having lost interest in the story that they already knew so well.

"When he made the scarecrow, Mr Grundy had no idea what he had created from the living material he found in Bluebell Wood, and with the old clothes he and his wife found in their cottage attic. It was by bringing together those particular old clothes and our special pole that enabled Mr Fudge could be created in the way he is: a speaking scarecrow with a human spirit. Can you imagine how pleased we were when he was placed in the potato field near our home in Bluebell Wood? He scares off the rooks during the day, keeps guard for us every night and does both jobs very well."

"That's an amazing story," she said as she continued to wonder why she and William had been so privileged to be let into these incredible secrets.

"But I'm a human being," she said to him, "and so is William, sometimes," she added with a smile.

"Oh yes, we know you are, but then you two are very special young humans, being friends of Mr Fudge. So, we know you won't harm us and that's the special reason you have been chosen to learn about us and to share our secrets."

A frown appeared on her face as she thought about that last statement, 'a very special reason'.

"There is an even more important reason than that for us to want to be friends with you and William," he continued, revealing a slight amusement in his gravely voice.

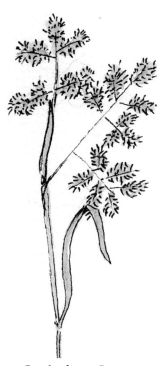

Cocksfoot Grass

"What's that?" she asked, eager to hear his answer.

"Mr Fudge let it be known, through Benjamin, that you are especially kind to animals and you look after your two guinea pigs at home. You clean them out regularly, you feed and water them when they need it, and on most days you play with them in your playroom."

There was a moment's silence before Lucy answered shyly, "Not always." She felt a little embarrassed, "Sometimes we forget and then Daddy has to do it for us, and it annoys him when he's busy with other things."

Her companion looked at her and said quietly, "Lucy, we know what goes on at Beech House, so if we hear that you are kind to your pets and Benjamin tells us that you help your Daddy, then we will let you into more secrets about the countryside and about us the next time you visit Rose Cottage Farm. As a very special treat, we might even teach you both how to see in the dark."

"See in the dark! Oh I will!" Lucy said excitedly. "I will make sure that we keep our pets warm, safe and well fed," she promised with a big smile on her face, which pleased everyone watching and listening to her.

"But what did you mean when you said that we had been selected for a very special reason?"

There was no response. The conversation was over and she would have to wait until the next time before she would find out what he meant.

During the months that followed, Lucy and William became frequent visitors to the underground cavern. Lucy loved to talk and play with the Little People and she taught them how to make necklaces from dried grass that they collected in the wood. She showed them how to fashion coloured beads from stones they found in the stream near the Roman Bridge. She even taught them how to dance, although the little ones had such short legs and clumsy feet that they kept falling over. It made her laugh so much that they all fell about in hysterics.

Timothy Grass

She taught them how to sing, although it required a great deal of effort and they were never in key. But they loved to try and they produced sounds that were almost like singing.

It wasn't only Lucy who visited the Little People. On other occasions, unknown to her, and especially during the summer months when no one was around and the moon shone brightly all night, William would make for the wood on his own to meet some of the younger male Little People.

He taught them how to play football with a ball he brought from home, and rugger which they enjoyed more because they could tussle and fight amongst themselves in the clearing around the stump. It wasn't real fighting, of course, just having good fun chasing each other. William tried to introducing them to cricket but their long hair and short arms proved too much of a disadvantage, so most nights were spent chatting and playing football in the clearing.

During the colder autumn and winter months, when it was too wet and frosty to play outside in the open, he would tell them about the complicated toy models he made at home from bits of balsa wood, cardboard and glue. The Little People knew nothing of model making and they were fascinated as he described how the models were made, first reading the instructions and then following the drawings. They had no idea what he meant by 'drawings and instructions', but by using the pencil that he always carried with him and a scrap of paper, he quickly showed them what a drawing looked like. It was clear to him that he would need to talk to Lucy about the possibility of teaching them to read.

On another occasion he told them about a toy boiler that Papo T had given him for Christmas. They didn't understand the meaning of Christmas but soon grasped the concept of a machine that could produce light. "It's a mechanical machine," he told them, "not like the fireflies in the cavern that are live insects and need to be fed."

In the mornings as they crossed the yard to the cottage for breakfast, he and Lucy would tell each other what they had been doing with their friends on their visits to the cavern.

Lucy kept a small diary, just like Papo's, in which she would write up these stories and events. Of course their mummy and daddy did not read them, but I don't think if they had done, they would have believed for one minute what went on in Bluebell Wood.

Chapter 6

A Midnight Feast

Sadly the holidays were drawing to an end again, with only one more day to enjoy the freedom and open space around the farm. Next week it would be back to school, meeting their best friends and telling them about their latest adventures in Dorset. Of course, there would be some things that William and Lucy would keep to themselves, those very special secrets that they had promised Mr Fudge and Benjamin would never be told.

However, Lucy and William had agreed with Mr Fudge and Benjamin that some things should be told to their parents.. It hadn't been easy to reach agreement.

"The time's not right yet," declared Mr Fudge in a rather pompous tone when they broached the subject with him. But eventually he agreed that the grown-ups would need to be told about some things quite soon.

Lucy lay on her bunk bed, hands behind her head, looking up at the white ceiling of their small room, day-dreaming about their meetings with the Little People. There were still so many unanswered questions about them that she wondered if she would ever find out the real truth. Were all these adventures in her imagination, or were they real? It couldn't be her imagination playing tricks because William was experiencing the same things and it couldn't happen to both of them at the same time, could it?

She couldn't ask William, who had already gone to sleep and was breathing steadily. For once he wasn't snoring, which he did when he got excited about things.

Deep down in her heart she knew he was also looking forward to getting home and seeing their parents, although all day yesterday he was mumbling about not wanting to go home just yet because he still had important things to do at the cavern. Lucy wondered what these things were, because he hadn't said a word to her earlier when they undressed for bed, and this was the time at the end of a day when they usually shared their thoughts.

Early autumn is the time of the year when the evenings slowly draw in, bringing the feeling that summer is coming to an end, but not quite yet. During the day, if there's not too much cloud around and the wind is blowing off the sea, there is a warmish feeling in the air. The sun is out and there is no need to wrap up in winter coats. It is at night that it turns cold.

From her top bunk, if Lucy craned her neck, she could see out of the window between the half-closed curtains. The pale moon looked huge as it lit up the night sky above the Dutch barn and threw watery shadows across the empty yard.

That evening before supper, Mr Grundy tuned into the weather forecast on the old radio that sat on the kitchen sideboard. He listened as they reported a high pressure system coming up the Channel. It would bring warm weather for the next few days. William looked at Lucy and winked as if to say, it should be all right for tonight and the party with our friends.

The last night of the holidays had arrived too quickly but it would be a fine one, with no rain to spoil their planning. They were going to join their friends in the potato field as a guest of Mr Fudge for a midnight feast. There was at least another hour before they had to get up. William's steady snoring kept Lucy awake and her mind filled with many thoughts. She wondered how many of the the Little People would venture out of the cavern to cross Upper Meadow to the party in the the potato field.

The silence of the room was suddenly interrupted by the loud screech of a nearby owl and was immediately answered by another call from an owl that Lucy guessed was some way off. It must be a family out hunting for their late supper, she thought. In the quiet that followed the disturbance her thoughts turned to home and how much she missed her parents. She was looking forward to seing them again and telling of their adventures, even though some stories would have to be kept secret for the time being.

As she and William had got older they did more things together as a family, not that they didn't do it before, but now it meant more to her. She was growing up and enjoyed doing things together. Cooking with Mummy was great fun and if Daddy wasn't flying, then helping him in the garden or cleaning out the pets was something she looked forward to sharing with him.

There were times on holiday when she felt a little homesick. She couldn't talk to Mrs Grundy about it and her husband certainly wouldn't understand, but she had William to keep her company and to remind her of home and he was a great comfort to her. He was always fun to be with. She often thought as she looked at him across the table during meal times, how lucky she was to have a brother who loved her so much and wanted to play and do things with her.

She remembered what Mr Fudge had said to her one day when he had realised that she was feeling a bit homesick. "Lucy," he said, "families, whether they're human ones or wildlife ones, are the most important thing that can happen to anyone or anything. They must stay firmly together through thick or thin, whatever happens." She had never though about it like that before, but being down here on the farm away from home, even with the nicest people you could ever meet, she realised what the dear old scarecrow was trying to tell her: families are the most important things in our lives.

With Mr Fudge's wise words ringing in her head, her thoughts returned to what was going to happen later that night. The Leader of the Little People had suggested the midnight feast. "We'll have it before our two human friends return home", he said. He also suggested that if they held it at the potato field, then Mr Fudge could join them, where he was happiest, standing guard. The potato crop had been lifted some months before and sold in the local market and so he had nothing to actually to guard, but he loved scaring the rooks for the fun of it and agreed that his potato field was an ideal spot for a midnight feast.

She realised it would be a dangerous journey for the Little People, crossing the grass fields at night, not because of the dark which they could see in, but because Mr Grundy might decide to go shooting that night. He often ventured out late at night The last thing anyone wanted tonight was for him to find a group of strange Little People crossing his land. It was unlikely that he would mistake them for game and take a shot at them, but they couldn't take that risk.

William stirred in the bottom bunk, just as Lucy heard the owls again, calling to each other in the distance. The sound jolted her back to consciousness and she was convinced that she hadn't slept a wink. Looking at her watch in the dark, the luminous hands pointed to eleven o'clock. Rubbing her eyes, she realised it was time to get up and out of bed. Still half asleep, she struggled into her jeans and jumper before shaking William to wake him. He protested at first, but then opened his eyes and realised it was time for yet another adventure to start.

He dressed quickly, slipping on his jeans and dark blue jumper, which was his favourite because it would keep him nice and warm. He didn't want to put on his coat, but Lucy insisted.

"It's cold outside William, so pleeeease put it on," she pleaded, just like their mother.

As he did so, he thought that he was always giving in to her, just to keep the peace. He found his shoes under the bed and put them on as quietly as he could.

"Come on William, we mustn't be late. Let's try and get there before the Little People arrive," his sister said as they made for the bedroom door. As they pulled the door quietly shut behind them, they saw the moon casting its long shadows across the yard, making dark shapes of the wheat stacks and the Dutch barn.

William followed his sister out of the building but with his eyes still unaccustomed to the semi-darkness, he nudged the dustbin with his foot and sent it sprawling. Luckily he caught it before it hit the ground and he put it back into position beside the door.

"Phew, that was lucky," he murmured to himself. Mr Grundy must have put it back too close to the door after emptying the contents into his tractor's trailer. Once a week he took the cottage waste and farm rubbish to dump into a deep pit at the other side of Bluebell Wood. It wasn't what you would call a proper rubbish dump, but local farmers had been using it for generations. No one really minded as it was situated several miles from the nearest dwelling.

The wheat stacks in the yard

From the cottage a faint purring sound came through an open window. Lucy tightened her grip on Williams's hand.

"Can you hear that noise William?" she asked in a whisper.

He did. "I think it's either Mr Grundy snoring or ..." and his voice trailed off as more noises came from behind the barn, louder and more distinctive than the first. Walking faster, they opened the yard gate and looked towards the hen house from where the noises were coming from.

They didn't have to wait long to find out what all the fuss and commotion was about. There in front of them was a fox, trying very hard to crawl under the wooden hen house. One of this year's litter, Lucy thought as it turned, stopped what it was doing, looked at them and then shot off towards Bluebell Wood and safety.

"It's a pity Mr Grundy isn't around with his gun right now," said William, "It would be a good opportunity to get rid of another of those foxes that have been causing so much trouble with the hens this summer."

"Yes, I know," said Lucy quietly under her breath. "Mrs Grundy told me the other day that they've lost twenty hens already this summer. Any more and they will have to buy some new ones to replace them." Although she didn't like shooting foxes, she understood why you can't let foxes have their way completely. Who wants to loose all their hens?

"It's not only hens that they kill," said William. "Do you know they will also attack newly born lambs?"

That's true, she thought, as they turned away from the hen house and walked silently towards the potato field, happy that this time the fox had got away without being shot and that Mrs Grundy hadn't lost another laying hen.

It was a beautiful, warm night. There was no wind to disturb the high branches or rustle the leaves as they made their way across Lower Meadow towards the potato field.

"Come on William, keep close to me and try not to make too much noise," Lucy insisted as he quickened his pace to catch up with her, seeing her easily in the moonlight that cast weird shapes on the damp grass.

They were about half way across the meadow and keeping close to the fence, when suddenly they were surprised by a ghostly swooshing sound behind them. A large owl flew silently past them, so low that it nearly touched William with its wings. They watched as it landed, feet outstretched, in the long grass just to their right. The ghostly grey shape rose out of the grass on silent wings clutching a wriggling, squeaking shrew in its talons. As silently and as quickly as it arrived, it disappeared in the dusk, flying off towards the farm buildings.

"A large owl flew silently past them, its talons outstretched"

They froze in their tracks and Lucy grabbed William's arm.

He realised how scared she was and tried to comfort her by putting an arm around her shoulder.

"It's alright," he said reassuringly. "Its gone, but it really frighten me, Lucy, until I realised what it was."

"Me too," she gasped, "I think it's one of those barn owls from the Dutch barn looking for its supper."

"I know. He won't hurt us if he comes back, but he's more likely to go hunting somewhere else now that he knows we're here."

The wooden gate into Mr Fudge's potato field was half open. Even in the dark, they didn't have to look too hard to see him standing in his usual place, upright and proud, the best scarecrow in the county.

"Hello Fudge," William called out excitedly as they approached him.

"Mr Fudge to you young man," he answered sternly, putting William in his place, but they could see that he was pleased to see them, even if he did sound a bit gruff.

For the average, run-of-the-mill scarecrow, it can get pretty lonely at night, standing in an empty field with nothing to scare away. However, there were always a few field mice playing around the base of the pole and perhaps a mole, bold enough to come above ground for a sniff. Moles normally catch their main food, earthworms, underground but just occasionally, a mole might catch a fat worm out of its burrow, hunting for leaves to pull down into their worm holes.

However, for a very special scarecrow like Mr Fudge, it can be very boring with no one to talk to and nothing big to scare away, and so as he stood waiting for the first arrivals he hoped that tonight would be different.

"Have you seen Benjamin on your walks from the farm, Lucy?" he asked, slightly agitated when she came towards him.

"No we haven't, but we were scared on the way here tonight by one of the barn owls that swooped down and really frightened us," she replied.

"Benjamin should have been here at midnight to start the feast. I asked him not to be late, especially not tonight of all nights," he mumbled aloud so that both of them could just hear what he said.

Lucy did her best to reassure him that they would soon be here. "Maybe they didn't want to come away from their cavern, even for a special feast," she said, hoping that she would be wrong.

Long minutes passed without a word being spoken. As he stood waiting by the gate in the semi-darkness, William noticed a faint movement in the direction of the wood. He thought it might be another evening prowler, but then in the moonlight he saw a group of Little People walking closely down the lee of the overgrown hedge towards them. They were being led by Benjamin and their Leader..

"They're here!" he shouted and went to meet them, greeting them like lost friends. They crowded around him, slapping him on the back and tugging at his arm as he led them through the gate towards a slightly impatient Mr Fudge.

Looking around her, Lucy thought there must be at least thirty of their cavern friends in the group, ready to enjoy the feast. She went around them, hugging the one she knew and saying hello to others she hadn't met before.

With all the chatter and happy activity around him, it took Benjamin a few moments to gain control.

"Let's have some order here please," he demanded at the top of his voice, as he turned to three of the larger Little People and asked them to lay out the feast.

"Before we know it," he reminded them,"it will be light and we must get back before the sun rises."

"Why?" asked Lucy.

"I don't really know," he answered, "but it's something we have always done, as long as I've known the Little People. Why don't you go and ask their leader, Lucy?"

By the light of the stars that shone down onto the potato field, casting dancing shadows here and there, the Little People took their places in a circle facing inwards towards Mr Fudge. The Leader, sitting close to Benjamin, asked William and Lucy to join him. They did so, knowing what an honour it was to be treated in such a way by the Leader. William vaguely remembered being told in history lessons at school that in ancient times, honoured guests at feasts would be asked to sit next to the chieftain or king.

He couldn't believe his eyes as all the goodies appeared, as if from nowhere. Although he had eaten one of Mrs Grundy's wholesome suppers, his mouth watered as he gazed on the array of delicate foods placed in front of them.

Stacked on large green leaves, similar to rhubarb leaves, were piles of succulent fruity blackberries, surrounded by plump brown crispy hazel nuts. Another leaf was crammed high with large strawberries, bigger than Lucy had ever seen. On another leafy plate some delicious newly baked fairy cakes caught William's eye. He wondered where it all came from as they all tucked in, politely allowing Lucy, William and Benjamin to have the first taste.

It seemed from what the Leader was saying to them that most of the food had been stored underground after it had been picked earlier in the summer. They didn't make fire to cook with, but had perfected the art of storing fruit, nuts and other vegetables from the countryside so that they had sufficient supplies to last them throughout the year.

Benjamin explained that unlike the foods that humans eat, the cavern dwellers had no need for meat and that the ordinary fields and local woodlands had provided the fantastic array of plants and fungi that was laid out before them.

"Benjamin," said Lucy, "I remember we were told at school by our teachers, and by Mummy and Daddy, that we need to eat protein as well as carbohydrates to stay healthy."

"That's absolutely true," he replied as he munched another handful of mixed nuts. "The Little People know all about eating properly. One day they might just tell you about it if you ask them, but not tonight Lucy, OK?"

Under the twinkling lights of the autumn night, the party ate until they were full and could hardly stand up. Out of the corner of his eye William noticed that Mr Fudge, who had been very quiet all evening, had not eaten a morsel.

"Aren't you hungry?" he asked him without thinking. "This food is so good that I've eaten too much. You'd like it too."

"I don't eat food William. I'm just an ordinary scarecrow made out of straw, old clothes, a few bits of wood and a turnip for a head, with no real mouth or eyes. I can understand and speak to humans like you two, but I can't walk and I can tell you that those are real drawbacks. So I suppose that makes me a very special scarecrow doesn't it, not just an ordinary one?"

"Sorry," said William, completely forgetting that Mr Fudge had no real mouth like he did, and that he would be hurt by his unthinking comments. Stupid me, he quietly thought to himself, saying nothing for a while as he thought about the scarecrow standing in front of him.

"I know you are an ordinary scarecrow on the outside, Mr Fudge, but you know that you are a very special friend to Lucy and me and we do love you very much, don't we

"A very special scarecrow, not just an ordinary one"

Lucy?" He turned towards his big sister for reassurance .

"Of course we do," she replied looking into Mr Fudge's eyes and seeing a slight hint of recognition. "Meeting you and Benjamin, then meeting all these lovely friends of yours has changed our lives completely. Do you know that at the end of each day, William and I talk about what's happened to us and all the things we've done, then I write it all down in my diary, like Papo who keeps a daily diary, although we've never seen it, have we William?"

"No, but one day I'm going to ask him if I can look at it."

The Little People ate quietly, listening intently to this conversation. As William finished talking they got up and clapped, stamped their feet and hugged him and Lucy, because in the countryside, friendship is important to everyone and they had grown to like their two young human friends very much.

When the feast was finished and the left-overs carefully cleared away, a few of the older Little People recalled life in the cavern and told stories of the past history of their tribe. Throughout the evening their leader said very little, he was happy to let the younger ones have their way.

Lucy danced for them and made them laugh when she pulled her funny faces and William sang a rugby song. Soon they were all dancing around in circles and singing in their squeaky voices. To everyone's delight, Benjamin and Mr Fudge joined in the singing, rather out of tune, but their efforts made everyone laugh even more. Never in the long history of Rose Cottage Farm had there been such a party in the potato field.

Eventually, with everyone exhausted, the Leader stood up, waving an arm to get attention. Turning, he said to Benjamin, "It's going to be light soon, the sun will rise above Bluebell Wood and we must all get back to the cavern before it's too late."

He looked at William and Lucy and they could just make out a smile from under his hairy face. "Thank you both for being our friends. I believe this friendship will turn into something far greater than we can possibly imagine," he said, looking at Benjamin.

"Please Leader, we want to thank you for this wonderful feast," William called out, choking back a strange feeling in the back of his throat that he had never experienced before.

"What do you think he meant Sis, 'something greater'?" he asked as he stared at the Leader, who was walking towards Benjamin.

"I don't know William. Maybe we should ask Mr Fudge, but not tonight because I have a feeling he wants us all to go now."

There was very little mess to clear up. All the rubbish from their feasting had been stacked away in two wicker baskets that Benjamin said he would hide at the farm, but didn't tell them where.

"Benjamin said he would hide the baskets at the farm ... but didn't say where."

With a wave to their friends, Lucy and William left the little group, as Benjamin gathered the Little People together so that he could escort them back to the clearing. Walking briskly, the youngsters soon arrived back at Rose Cottage Farm without meeting anyone or anything, not even the barn owl.

At breakfast next morning, having got up later than usual, they noticed that Mr Grundy was a bit agitated. It wasn't because his fried egg was too hard or his bacon too crispy, it was for another reason all together. He told them that when he came down to make tea for his wife, long before they were up, he noticed that the kitchen door had not been locked the night before. It was a job that he did religiously every night before going to bed. He was adamant that he had locked it before going to bed last night.

Lucy looked up from her cereals at William, who could hardly stifle a grin as they looked across the table towards Mr Grundy. So that's where the cakes came from!

Chapter 7

The Storm

Lucy and William returned home to Beech House with many tales to tell their parents about their stay at Rose Cottage. So much had happened but some things had to stay secret, at least for now.

Settling back into school took a bit of adjustment. There were classes to attend every morning and homework to do every evening. They had also promised Mr Fudge that they would look after their pets, instead of expecting Daddy doing it. Then there was boring housework, not that they did much of that, but keeping the playroom tidy was a 'must do' job, as their mother had so many other things to do .

It was Wednesday night at Rose Cottage. The Grundys were missing the young ones, and Mr Grundy had had a very busy week on the farm. He wanted to get some of the hedges in the bottom field tidied up before the bad weather settled in. Hedge tidying was an important job after the busy summer work but it was not easy. In fact, Mr Grundy hated this time of the year. It was neither summer nor winter as far as he was concerned, but the jobs had to be done, whatever the weather.

The only good thing about cold weather at this time of the year was looking forward to his evening meal. He loved his wife's cooking, especially if it was a pork casserole that she made from a tasty chunk of prime meat cut off one of their cured joints that hung on the hooks in the kitchen. It was cooked slowly in the Aga and liberally flavoured with herbs, some from their own garden. It made his mouth water just thinking about it, let alone smelling it as he took off his boots at the back door.

He thought that he must listen to the weather forecast after supper to get some idea of local conditions tomorrow. He could then decide whether to continue with the hedge laying. If the rain kept off, he could get another day's work done on the Lower Meadow hedge.

If only there was someone like young William or Lucy to help him, he thought, what a difference that would make. But they weren't around and he would have to get on with it on his own. Like all dedicated farmers he took pride in his work, even though there were some jobs that he didn't like. But like his father before him, he knew a tidy farm was always a successful one. As a boy it was drummed into him, so that now it was simply a habit in the way he ran the farm.

Hedge laying was an old farming skill. Every autumn he spent a few weeks tackling the more difficult hedges, those that had become too overgrown and where some of the older plants had died. This left gaps which had to be layered from the good growth on either side. It was the only way to rejuvenate the whole hedge other than replanting long stretches, which he didn't want to do because it took time and was expensive.

Although Mr Grundy didn't have sheep or cattle on the farm, he rented out some of his grass fields for grazing. Well-laid hedges were better than putting up posts and wire to keep the stock in the field. The other good thing about laid hedges was that they provided good cover for pheasants and partridge, and nesting places for the smaller birds.

Cleaning up hedges is an autumn job which we know he doesn't like doing very much because it could be cold and sometimes it rained quite hard. If the wind got up he had difficulty cleaning up the loose brushwood that piled up

after he cut, trimmed and layered the hedges. But this autumn the weather had been milder. There were warm days when he enjoyed working in the fields and then there were others when it rained hard and he had to find jobs to do in the sheds, or paperwork in the kitchen. Then he hated getting under his wife's feet as she went about her chores, especially on a Wednesday which was always her baking day.

This Wednesday was going to be like any other autumn day, with lots of work to do and no one to help him. The alarm went off at 6 a.m. as usual. He washed without waking his wife and he didn't have to shave. He'd worn a beard for the last twenty years and was now quite used to it. Putting on a thick vest under his shirt, he was about to slip on his trousers when his wife woke and murmured something about getting up to make his breakfast for him. Standing by the end of their bed he slipped a thick brown jumper over his head. It was the one his wife hated because of all the holes that adorned it. Not to worry! It was his hedge laying jumper and ideal for doing that type of job in this type of weather.

As he walked towards the kitchen he wondered why wives hate old clothes, "I'll never understand them," he murmured to himself. "Bless them."

By 7.30 a.m. he had eaten a lovely cooked breakfast of three rashes of crispy bacon cut from the large joint hanging in the corner, two fried eggs, done to a turn, a slice of fried bread cooked to a golden crispy brown in the bacon fat, and two tomatoes to complement it all.

Mrs Grundy always insisted that he have a good breakfast before going out in the cold weather, especially at this time of the year. His meal was washed down with a large cup of steaming coffee, laced with plenty of sugar. No need for toast and marmalade this morning. Enough was enough.

Over the years certain personal habits had grown between them that they both accepted with great pleasure. There was always strong coffee for breakfast, old-fashioned tea for lunch most days and special tea at the weekends when they had time to relax and enjoy it.

He loved his mug of coffee in the mornings before going out to work in the fields. Today was no exception, but he wasn't to know that this particular day would be full of surprises, some not to his liking at all.

"Don't forget your lunch, will you dear?" his wife called out. "It's on the table by the back door near your boots." It was always on the table by the back door, in the same place, that's why he loved her so much. She never let him down. She always did that and said the same thing, because like Papo, Mr Grundy was a bit forgetful and needed to be reminded sometimes if he had a lot on his mind. Today was no exception.

He missed not having the children around and spent a lot of time thinking about the mystery they had set him, but most of all, he still hadn't found out what the two of them got up to when away from the cottage. This happened quite frequently on their last visit. Ah well, he thought, no doubt they'll tell me soon enough, and he made his way towards the barn to collect his hedging gear.

He left by the back door, closing it behind him. Looking up, he was surprised by the chatter and squawking that the rooks were making as they circled high above Bluebell Wood. Something is worrying them this morning, he thought, but dismissed it as he entered the Dutch barn to pick up his axe and thick leather gloves from the bench, and the

The rook, keeping watch

slasher that he always propped up next to the metal cupboard. I mustn't forget that sharpening stone, he told himself as he looked on top of the shelf where he kept his small tools and other bits and pieces.

He smiled to himself, thinking that the weather forecast was right and it was going to be a pleasant day with high clouds coming in off the sea. A good day for working at the hedges.

Passing through the farm yard he opened the gate, looked over towards the hens that were pecking away at the soil, completely oblivious to his presence. He turned left and shouldering his tools and lunch in his bag, made for the hedge on the west side of Lower Meadow.

He passed Mr Fudge, standing proudly in the empty potato field and he thought that he must go and have a look at him later, just in case he needed a bit more padding out with straw. The scarecrow had been there all summer and there was bound to be some repair work to do. I'll do it tomorrow without fail, he said to himself as he approached the hedge that he would be working on today.

He placed his lunch bag against the roots of an old elm tree and as he did so his attention was drawn towards Bluebell Wood. The noisy rooks were

Mr Fudge was alert to their tricks

playing up more than usual, falling around the sky and calling to each other as if they were warning of some danger. Something is definitely worrying them, he thought, but I don't know what.

At this time of the morning the sky was almost clear of clouds, the wind was pleasant and didn't give him cause for concern. Maybe there's a litter of foxes prowling around near to their rookery, he mused, knowing that would certainly create havoc amongst the resident flock. I must tell Mrs Grundy that the vixen has appeared again and warn her to keep the hens in at night, he said to himself as he examined the length of hedge to be laid. I'd prefer to eat the hens myself than let that sly old fox get them.

Putting on his thick leather gloves he gave the short bladed slasher a few quick flicks with the 'stone' to give it a really sharp edge, then did the same with the blade of the axe. Past experience told him that working on a hedge with sharp tools was much easier than with tools that were even slightly blunt. Sharpening tools was a job that gave him a great deal of pleasure, not because it took a lot of skill to get that perfect edge, but because the cuts they made in the stems and trunks of the hedge and bushes were clean, and clean wounds healed quicker.

During the early part of the morning the rooks continued their squawking as they whirled and generally made a nuisance of themselves. Once or twice a fight broke out and groups of the birds flew down to the empty potato field. They obviously hoped to snatch a few rotting potatoes left behind after the harvest, but they were without much luck. Others had already been there before them.

Mr Fudge was alert to their tricks and although he couldn't wave his arms about, the noise he made was enough to frighten away the hardiest and bravest of them.

This surprised Mr Grundy as he looked up from sharpening his tools. How did his scarecrow frighten off the rooks? Of course, Mr Grundy hadn't heard Mr Fudge shout out because only the rooks were able to hear him. They knew very well not to cross him when he was in one of his dark moods.

For a couple of hours the work went well. It was mid-morning and time for his break. As he sat on his old jacket drinking from the cup of the thermos flask and thinking about the work so far completed, he saw a flock of wood pigeons flying fast and low from the direction of the old ruined mill. There were pigeons about most days, visiting the farm buildings or scavenging in the potato field, but he had seldom seen so many fly so fast before, all winging their way towards Bluebell Wood. If only he had his gun with him, but then they were flying far too fast for a shotgun.

With the unusual noise of the rooks and now seeing the pigeons fly overhead, he wondered to himself as he scratched his head, something is definitely up and I wish I knew what it was. Dismissing the thought from his mind, he finished his coffee, put the empty flask back into his bag and returned to the next bit of hedge to be worked on.

When you look at him and his grey beard, Mr Grundy gives the impression of being a bit gruff, but in fact he is a very gentle man. As he worked at the hedge, slashing at the unwanted branches, cleaning out the old brushwood, selecting the thin trunks that he wanted to keep as the skeleton of the new hedge, he whistled quietly to himself. It was a hedge laying tune that his father had taught him when he was a young lad. Although it didn't rhyme, the words described the art of hedge laying:

When you lay a hedge, cut out
The dead and weedy branches,
Clean out the bottom of the hedge,
Select the strong branches and cut them at the base,
Then bend them over without snapping them off.
Lay the branches in the same direction,
About 45 degrees to the ground.

To keep them upright and animal proof
Put a straight pole upright through the layered hedge
And into the ground.
To finish off, take the thin branches that were cut off,
Twist them into a rope and wind round the upright poles.
That's the job done.

The poem doesn't rhyme one little bit but that didn't matter to him, as it always brought back happy memories of hours in the fields working alongside his dad. It was at times like this that he wished he and his wife had children. That wasn't to be, but they could look forward to Lucy and William visiting them during the holidays. Their visits always brought back memories of his own happy childhood and gave him such pleasure.

He whistled quietly to himself. Both hands worked in unison, cutting, pointing and sharpening poles with his knife, whittling away at the good branches and twisting the little spindly ones into a living rope. The hours slipped by as he as he progressed down the old hedge so the new, beautifully layered hedge unfolded behind him as if by magic.

There was no wind about but he shivered as the clouds scuttled across the sky, chasing their tails as if there was a race to see who could cross Bluebell Wood first.

During a lull, he piled up the unused branches and twigs into small heaps, keeping them away from the new hedge and the trees that were dotted at intervals along the boundary. The twigs were so dry that there was no need for paper to help set them alight. They flared up and burnt quickly with very little smoke to annoy him. But then, there was no one near him to annoy anyway except himself.

The flames died out as quickly as they had flared up and the two piles of dead chopped hedge wood were soon reduced to grey smouldering ash. A job well done, he thought as he looked down the remaining hedge and weighed up how long it would take to finish the final stretch. Might get it completed tomorrow if the weather stays as it has today, he thought to himself, pleased with the results so far.

The rest of the morning sped by. He was so engrossed in his work that he had soon completed about forty feet of laying since he started that morning. This was good going, considering that he was on his own and couldn't work as fast as he used to when he was a younger man.

The hard work made him hungry and finding a dry spot on the ground beside the hedge, he opened his lunch box. A big smile lit up his face as he saw

"The beautifully layered hedge unfolded behind him"

the packed lunch that his wife had made for him. There were two large ham sandwiches with his favourite chutney and mustard, a small round pork pie that his wife made from cured ham and bacon, an apple from the store room and a chocolate bar. He ate them without a care in the world, day-dreaming about the best laid hedge in the county. I wonder if it would get a prize? he thought.

But then, Oh no, dear me, guess what? He had forgotten to pick up the black flask of tea from the kitchen table. This was serious, as he had to have his tea after lunch. Lunch wouldn't be lunch without his cup of tea. What was he to do?

He could either walk back to the cottage to collect the flask or he could wait and make up for it at teatime. In the end he decided to finish the job early. The work had certainly gone well today and he'd achieved a good run of hedge laying. If the weather is as good as this tomorrow, it wouldn't matter if I finish early today, he told himself. The rubbish was all burnt so he was pleased with his efforts.

No sooner had he finished eating his lunch and packed his bag, then the sky changed dramatically, growing very dark and overcast. Thick dark grey clouds appeared from behind the hills near the lake. The rooks had vanished and all around him it became very still as the sky turned from dark grey to black-as-the-ace-of-spades. He knew immediately that he must get home quickly before the storm clouds opened up. I should have known better, he thought, when I recognised the early signs of this storm brewing. The agitated rooks and the racing pigeons were signs he should have recognised, but it was too late now and he would be drenched to the skin within the next few minutes.

It happened fast. One minute he was bending down, clearing up his tools, and next moment the heavens opened above him. The noise was frightening as the rain thundered on the ground. The wind ripped off his cap and glasses and he struggled to stand upright. Then without warning, a dead branch of

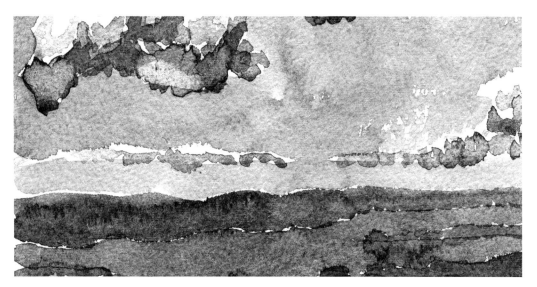

The sky changed dramatically, growing very dark and overcast

the elm tree above him crashed to the ground, clipping him on the shoulder. He was knocked to the ground, stunned but still conscious, to find his arm pinned by the weight of the branch. He was unable to move and was already soaked through.

Calm soon turned to fear. What was he going to do? He couldn't move and who would find him out here? How could he get a message to his wife, who wouldn't worry about him until it was dark and he still hadn't arrived home? There were many evenings when he was late and she was used to keeping his supper warm in the Aga. He regretted not having a mobile phone, which they had decided was an unnecessary expense.

However, like so many storms at this time of the year, it passed over as quickly as it arrived. The rain stopped and the black clouds moved on. But Mr Grundy couldn't move. The branch was too heavy to budge and his arm was becoming numb and cold. He felt quite helpless. He had no idea of the time, but it must have been a couple of hours after the disaster struck that he lost consciousness.

The sun had dropped below the horizon and back at Rose Cottage, Mrs Grundy was becoming worried. It was unusual for her husband to stay out as late as this during the early autumn evenings, unless he told her beforehand that he would be late coming home. He liked to get into the warm kitchen before it turned cold, and sup a mug of tea in front of the Aga. This time of the year he always warned his wife if he was going to be late home.

Flying low and following the line of the hedge from the direction of Bluebell Wood, was one of this year's young barn owls. Hunting during the early evening was normally very successful and during the last four months he had developed his skills to a high level. He was searching for shrews, who also ventured out looking for their supper at this time of day, and for the field mice, enjoying the early dampness of the grass. The undergrowth of the unlaid hedge was also home to the voles that barn owls are particularly partial to. However, voles are quick on their feet and normally escape the swooping talons of the owls.

As he glided like a ghost on silent wings just above the level of the hedge, the owl noticed Mr Grundy lying under the fallen branch, pinned to the ground and so still he could have been dead. Realising that he must be hurt, the young owl flew down the hedge towards the potato field. He landed on Mr Fudge's outstretched arm and told him what he had seen.

"This is an emergency," cried Fudge in a language that owls understood. "I need to get Benjamin to help us. Please fly off to the farm and find him. Don't delay to catch mice on the way, this errand is urgent."

Benjamin was having a quiet supper in his den behind the Dutch barn when the barn owl swooped down and landed on the table. He indicated in the sign language that Mr Fudge had taught him that he wanted Benjamin to follow him to the potato field. There was an emergency and his help was needed, right now.

Benjamin hurried to the potato field, where he quickly hatched a plan with Mr Fudge and their friend the barn owl. They would need the help of the Little People to move the big tree branch before they could try to carry Mr Grundy back to the farm. But if he regained consciousness, would he allow them to help? He had not seen them before and even humans might be afraid of strange looking hairy creatures like the Little People.

"We'll have to take that risk," said Mr Fudge, and Benjamin ran off towards Bluebell Wood as fast as he was able, to ask the Little People for their help. He quickly explained what had happened to Mr Grundy and

"He landed on Mr Fudge's arm"

without hesitation the Leader agreed to organise a small group of the tribe to assist in the rescue.

"We'll need everyone to help," they shouted excitedly and before you could blink an eye they were up the rickety stone steps, through the wood, across the meadow and were gathered at the scene of the accident.

Mr Grundy was still unconscious and very, very cold. His face was white under his beard and his lips were turning dark blue. The Leader and Benjamin gave instructions for lifting the branch and with a mighty heave the team managed to lift the branch off his arm. The others pulled him out very gently and as quickly as they dared to.

"Can you carry him to Rose Cottage?" asked Benjamin. "I'll show you the way and I suggest that when we get there, just prop him up by the back door of the cottage. Knock on the door loudly but don't wait. I'm sure his wife will know what to do when she opens the door."

The orders had been issued. It was getting very dark and the moon could just be seen above the ruined mill as eight Little People, helped by their Leader and guided by Benjamin, carried the unconscious Mr Grundy across Lower Meadow and back to Rose Cottage.

Because they were so apprehensive about humans, they did as Benjamin advised them to do. They left Mr Grundy propped up as comfortably as possible against the side of the back door. The Leader ushered the group towards the yard gate as he knocked on the door loud enough for Mrs Grundy to hear from her kitchen.

Drying her hands on a towel that rested on the side of the Aga, she pulled back the bolt at the top of the door, opened it and looked out into the evening dusk. What a surprise she got on opening the door. Her dear husband was struggling to get to his feet, dazed, very pale and extremely wobbly.

"What's happened, what's the matter with you dear? Where have you been all this time, are you hurt?" The questions poured out as she put her strong arms around him and helped him into the kitchen, sitting him down in front of the warm Aga. She saw the blood on his left hand and his shirt was covered in dirt and torn in several places.

Mr Grundy lay back in his comfy chair with his eyes closed, trying to speak but making no sense to his wife. She took off his cap, undid his shirt buttons and tried to ease it over his head. "Just look at you, what a mess you're in."

He was so pleased to be back home and in the warmth of his kitchen. "How did I get here?" he gasped .

"Don't worry about that right now, you just drink this warm tea," his wife said, as she passed him a mug of his favourite brew, straight from the pot.

"Dazed and extremely wobbly"

"Let me get you out of that torn shirt. You're cold and wet and I want to look at your arm and wash that blood off your hand. That wound on your arm could be more dangerous than it looks."

He drank the tea, laced with plenty of sugar and a touch of medicinal brandy, while she washed the blood off and carefully inspected the badly bruised arm. It wasn't the first time he'd hurt himself but this looked like the worst accident he'd had for some time.

"You know, you really must be more careful at your age," she chided him as she eased a freshly-ironed shirt over the hurt arm. "How you managed to get back home with all that pain I have no idea," she said lovingly, pleased that he was quickly getting back to his old self and asking for another cup of tea and something to eat. He must be feeling better, she thought to herself.

"Tell me all about it, from the very beginning please, and don't leave anything out. Now what happened dear?"

Over the next half hour he recalled the story about the day's work in as much detail as he could remember. How pleased he was and how well the hedge laying had progressed. He remembered enjoying his lunch and that he'd forgotten his flask of tea, which was a nuisance. He mentioned that he had thought about coming home but had changed his mind. Now he wished he hadn't.

He could remember being concerned about the noise the rooks had made, but had not given it too much thought. The pigeons were another indication of the storm to come, but he had dismissed them as well. Then as he relaxed and warmed himself in front of the Aga sipping his second cup of tea, it slowly came back to him. Of course, he remembered, there had been a sudden rain storm and a wind so strong that he could hardly stand upright. Then he remembered lying on the ground, pinned down by that rotten old branch, unable to move and being drenched to the skin as the rain lashed down on him. Then nothing.

He tried to remember but his mind was blank. He did remember getting cold, then passing out with the excruciating pain in his arm, but nothing else until he came to at the back door when his wife came to help him in.

"Don't you remember walking back across the fields?" she asked sympathetically.

"No, my mind's a complete blank. I didn't walk back, not as far as I can remember," he replied with a worried look appearing on his tired old face.

"If you didn't walk back on your own, then how could you have possibly made it back to the cottage across the fields dear?"

"I honestly don't know, I have no idea how I did it," he answered. "I might have been in a trance or someone might have helped me, but I have no idea who," he said. "Whoever it was, left me propped up against the back door and left quickly, obviously not wanting to be seen."

"It must have been someone," she replied with a puzzled look on her face, "because I'm sure I heard a knock at the back door. That's why I went to open it."

He had told his wife all that he could remember, but to this very day he has no idea how he managed to get himself home that day.

Chapter 8

The New Arrivals

For some time now William and Lucy had known that they were very lucky young people. They had two sets of grandparents who were still quite active considering how old they were. Well, they thought they were old, but in truth they only pretended to be old. Also, in a village called Flamstead, just north of London, lived their two young cousins, Thomas and Katie. They were both a few years younger than William and Lucy, but that didn't really matter.

Thomas was the happy smiling one, with blond curly hair. He was older than his sister Katie by a few years, but not by many. She was a tomboy, inquisitive, always wanting to know what was going on, and she tended to look after her older brother, but not in a bossy sort of way.

They loved to visit William and Lucy at Beech House, where they'd play hide and seek in the big garden or hide in the den and on especially warm days, eat picnic teas of crisps and sandwiches in the playhouse by the tennis court. In the summer, when it was really hot, Uncle Jack would erect a super large circular blue swimming pool that they all loved to play in. It was great fun, jumping into the water, splashing everyone who was near enough and ducking under the water to come up spluttering and coughing.

It was the Easter holiday and William and Lucy were visiting Rose Cottage on their own. Easter was late this year and the weather forecasters were correct for once in their predictions. It was warm most days and today was no exception. The gentle wind that appeared intermittently swirled around the valleys in Dorset, just strong enough to sway the early leaves on the trees and to provide powerful lift for soaring birds like the buzzards, who were continuously looking for prey. In many of the grass fields newly born lambs were enjoying the warm spring weather, playing their lamb games, jumping over their dozing parents and chasing each other around in circles, trying hard to grab each others' tails.

Although there were no lambs at Rose Cottage Farm, there were several flocks nearby and Mr Grundy often thought that it would be good to have a few sheep on the farm to help keep the grass down in the summer. Controlling grass growth was a problem for him most summers and when he was younger there had been a sheep flock on this farm.

With Mrs Grundy's agreement, William and Lucy had decided that today they would go for a picnic to the nearby lake. For once they wanted to be on their own with no grown-ups to boss them about, telling them what to do and what not to do. It wasn't that they didn't like grown-ups, but to be on your own would be a great treat, especially down here on the farm.

They could both swim very well but had promised Mr Grundy faithfully that whatever happened they would not venture too close to the lake side. Mr Grundy warned them that this year the lake was very muddy, particularly near the shoreline, due to the heavy spring rains falling a few months earlier on the inland moors. However, he was happy that they would behave themselves and not disobey him. You see, he trusted them because in the past when he had trusted them to do something they had kept their promise.

Although younger than his sister, William was the stronger of the two and he agreed to carry the picnic basket as it was rather heavy with all the lovely goodies Mrs Grundy had prepared for them for their tea. They knew it would be a treat because they had no idea what she had hidden in their basket, that's why picnics were such fun. Lucy decided that as William was going to carry the basket, she would carry the red tartan rug that they would spread out on the grass to use as a table.

Before leaving the cottage Mr Grundy gave them precise instructions on the best route to take, but it still took them nearly two hours to walk across two grass fields and the lower water meadows. They climbed through the gaps in old hedges and over two rickety broken down gates which hadn't been opened for years, before eventually arriving at the lakeside that Mr Grundy had told them about.

It was one of those beautiful balmy days in early summer. The countryside around them was peaceful but alive with the sound of insects. The still air was disturbed only by a few midges buzzing around to annoy them. Above them, high in the sky, a few fluffy white clouds ambled slowly across the pale blue emptiness. The silence was interrupted by the early summer songs of blackbirds, the background buzz of bees hunting for nectar and a solitary song thrush, somewhere in the woods off to their right. The wind had dropped and made barely a ripple on the water in the middle of the lake. By the lake shore, the line of gently swaying reed beds stretched either side of the stream outlet, which they knew was the same stream that passed the cottage and flowed under the Roman Bridge.

As they stood looking out towards the centre of the lake they were aware of a sudden water disturbance amongst the nearby reeds. There could be a single heron feeding there or maybe some water voles playing in and out of the rotten reeds that had succumbed to the previous winter's damage. The old reed stems lay twisted amongst the upright stems, providing a safe area for voles and other small creatures.

Over on the other side of the lake, they could just make out through the early summer haze two white sails of a small sailing boat. It seemed to be hardly moving on the still water. The lake surface was so calm and peaceful,

The Kingfisher

not like other Easters that they could remember, when gales had blown so hard no one wanted to venture out.

Coming back to their senses they looked to the left and right, eventually finding a clear patch of grass near to the water's edge, which wasn't too wet or covered by a blanket of daisies or dandelions. The last thing they wanted were lumps and bumps under the table rug.

Lucy laid out her tartan rug, expertly pulling the corners to make sure that there were no bumps and hillocks to upset the cups. William carefully took out the food from his basket, piece by piece, and laid them on the rug, making sure that there were no ants or other creepy crawlies anywhere to be seen. William didn't mind ants or things like that, but Lucy preferred to have her tea without unwanted guests crawling over her sandwiches or swimming in her fruit juice.

Their walk across the fields and water meadows to the lake had given them both a good appetite. Sitting cross legged, facing the water, they were soon munching away at beautifully cut egg and cress sandwiches. They dropped crumbs all over the rug, but that didn't matter. This was their picnic and there were no grown-ups telling them to be careful of this, and mind you don't spill that.

"A small sailing boat on the far side of the lake ..."

Soon most of the sandwiches had disappeared along with two bags of their favourite cheese and onion crisps, followed by bits of juicy, freshly peeled fruit. The picnic was finished off by scoffing down Mrs Grundy's baked cakes. There were two each, with white icing on the top and strawberry jam oozing out of the middle. They were delicious.

They were both full to bursting. "Let's lie down on the rug for a few minutes, Lucy, to let this full feeling of mine wear off," murmured William in a drowsy voice. "Then we can go exploring this part of the lake side." Mr Fudge had told them about the ruins of an old castle and they could just make out what was left of it, about half a mile away, hidden amongst tall trees. If they looked hard enough they could just make out a tall square tower poking its battlements through the surrounding trees that hid most of the rest of the ruin from sight.

"It's too far away for us to explore today," muttered Lucy sleepily. "We'll keep that for another day, but I would really like to see what's there. You never know, there might be secret tunnels that have not been seen by human beings for hundred of years."

"Don't be silly Lucy," he retorted, "I bet lots of people have been there." He didn't like to think his sister knew more than him about history things.

The whole countryside scene around them was deserted except for the sailing boat, which seemed a long way off but was slowly getting nearer to their side of the lake. There was no one else in sight, either on the lake or on the land. Over to their right, some distance away, there were a few sheep and several brown dairy cows grazing in the water meadow near to the stream outlet, their heads down, grazing on the young lush green grass. They wouldn't disturb them, and anyway, the two of them were old enough now to deal with these farm animals if the need arose.

As they lay on their stomachs on the rug watching the boat gradually moving across the water towards them, they couldn't help but notice the activity of the wildlife around them. A pair of graceful white adult swans glided silently past their spot on the bank, taking no notice of them at all, not even on the off-chance that there might have been some food left over from their picnic. They had other things on their mind.

"Maybe they are looking for a nest site," said William as he stood up to watch them glide past, becoming hidden on the other side of the reeds. As the swans disappeared from sight, a grey heron flew in on large outstretched wings, seemingly from nowhere. With extended legs it landed on the other side of the reeds where the swans had disappeared. The heron was no doubt hoping to catch his tea and did not notice Lucy and William sitting on the grass watching him, talking very quietly to each other.

He was a young bird with very striking, dark head feathers, lovely grey wings speckled with black, and a long tail. William wondered if it was the same bird that frequently visited the farm to fish by the old stone bridge. Mr Fudge had told them recently that some herons fly up to twelve miles from their heronry to look for food, so it could be him or one of his family.

Lucy gently nudged her brother and pointed towards the reeds where a group of chattering brown birds the size and colour of sparrows, but with white chest feathers, chased flies and

Herons

99

other small insects flitting between the reed stems. Remembering pictures in her bird book, Lucy whispered,

"Do you think they're Reed Warblers or Marsh Warblers?" It was quite difficult to tell because they all look alike. She was sorry she hadn't brought her bird book with her to check. "I'll bring the book the next time we visit this part of the lake, maybe when we explore the ruin," she said. "This time, I'll have to remember their colouring and look it up when we get home."

High in the sky on the other side of the lake, slowly soaring around in ever-wider circles, was a lone bird that William thought might be a buzzard or a kite. It seemed to be sailing effortlessly through the sky, occasionally flapping its wings to maintain height. If they concentrated hard they could just hear it's plaintive 'peeiou' call.

"There must be another one somewhere nearby," said William, "because they always hunt in pairs this time of the year." But as hard as they looked neither of them could find the bird's mate.

"Look," cried Lucy, pointing to the bird. As they looked up towards the clouds, the bird suddenly folded its wings and plunged towards the earth like a bullet. Then, just as quickly, it sailed upwards again then rolled and turned in the air, showing off its flying skills. It was breathtaking to watch and it reminded them of the Golden Eagle they had once seen in a TV programme.

"Gosh, that was fantastic," exclaimed William.

That afternoon when they left the cottage, Mrs Grundy made sure that they each had a large plastic bottle of apple juice to quench their thirst. Picnics and exploring were thirsty work. Apple juice was one of their favourite drinks and they had at least a small bottle of it every day. Today was no exception and the juice disappeared before you could say "Jack Butler".

"If we get really thirsty later on, we can fill the bottles from the stream over there, near the reeds," said William, swallowing down the last mouthful of juice and wiping his mouth with the back of his hand.

"All this walking and exploring really does make me thirsty," he said, turning to look at his sister. They knew the stream water would be safe to drink, because Mr Fudge had told them about this spot near the reed beds a few months ago, on their last holiday at the farm. It was another reason why they had decided to picnic there at the edge of the water meadow where they could fill their bottles. The cows and sheep were in a field away from the stream so they wouldn't be a problem.

"Let's go and do some more exploring," said Lucy, turning to look at her brother for agreement. "I've had enough rest for the time being, have you?"

"OK," said William, getting off the rug. But before she could utter another sentence they both stared at the reeds with their mouths wide open in amazement.

"Look at that!" shouted out a startled William, his eyes the size of saucers. There, in front of them, standing quite still and looking straight at them, was the strangest creature that they had ever seen in their lives.

The creature was pinkish red all over, from the end of its long spiky tail to the tip of its nose. It was about the size of a very large cat but unlike normal cats, it had a long neck with little spikes running up its back, ending on the top of its head. It had a kindly looking face with wide, half closed eyes, and a long snout with wide nostrils. As it stood there staring at them, they could just make out two short stubby wings on its back and a long tail that swished from side to side.

"I don't believe it, Lucy, it's a dragon!" exclaimed William, jumping up from the rug and turning to his sister, his face white with fear.

"It can't be, can it?" said Lucy, trying very hard to be brave in front of her brother but feeling queasy inside. "Dragons don't exist in real life, silly, only in books and fairy tales."

"This one certainly does," William said emphasising each word. "This one is very real." Then the little red dragon rose up on its long back legs and

waddled slowly towards them, mouth open and pale pink tongue hanging out to one side.

"Run!" shouted William to his sister, but neither could move a muscle. The creature wasn't at all frightened by the two children, both frozen to the spot.

The tension was suddenly broken. From the other side of the reed bed they heard a young voice shout out. "Happy, Happy, where are you Happy? Get back here at once. I'll count up to three. Do you hear me?"

From the other side of the reed bed came a young boy, the owner of the voice. He had a mop of fair hair.

"Thomas!" they shouted together, running towards him but making sure they kept away from the little pink dragon that was making a beeline for their picnic rug.

"What are you doing here by the lake? Is Katie with you? Where are Uncle Chris and Aunty Liz?"

Suddenly, there were so many questions to be asked and answered that no one noticed that the dragon was sitting on the rug, finishing off what was left of their tea. He ate everything, including the paper plates but stopped as William snatched away the plastic bottles, just in time.

Tom pushed past Lucy and went over to the creature, putting his arm around its neck. "Stop that Happy, right now, or I'll put your collar on and you don't like that, do you?" He smiled at his cousins to reassure them. Happy was a softy at heart, but would eat anything if given half a chance.

With the dragon now sitting quietly between them, the three talked and talked. Thomas explained that he and Katie were staying with their mother and father at a holiday bungalow in a village on the other side of the lake, not far from the sea. It had to be the sea because Chris liked to walk on the sand and fly his kite, and Mummy needed to be near the shops. They had been there for about a week and still had another week to go.

"Guess what though?" said Thomas, standing up and pointing towards the lake shore. "We were in that small sailing boat over there," he said, pointing to the small boat that they had seen earlier. Now the the bow was resting on the grass bank on the other side of the reeds and the sails were flapping gently in the breeze. That's why William and Lucy hadn't noticed them arrive until the dragon appeared and frightened them both.

In the meanwhile, guess who had eaten all the left-overs from tea, and who had his head stuck in the basket looking for more?

"I call him Happy," said Thomas, going up to the dragon and lifting him up so that William could pull the basket off his head. "You mustn't be afraid of him, he's really very tame. At home he lives under the bed in the spare room."

While all this chatter had being going on, Katie, Aunty Liz and Uncle Chris had scrambled out of the boat without getting their feet too wet and were now greeting, hugging and kissing everyone. They were all so pleased to see each other.

Uncle Chris looked around the grass site at their blanket and said "Now we're here, this is just the place to have our picnic," and he went back to the boat to take out a huge wicker hamper that he carried up the grass slope. Placing it down the rug he unfastened the straps and opened the lid. It was full to the brim with goodies.

Aunty Liz always made sure there was enough to go round twice, especially if Uncle Chris was with them. Lucy and William glanced at each other, winked and said, "Oh yes, please, Uncle Chris," even though they had just eaten their own huge picnic tea.

When you live in the country with all the fresh air, you are always hungry. Happy looked as if he could still manage a sandwich or two, having tried to eat the plastic plates before being stopped by Thomas.

They sat round on the rug, the dragon panting beside Thomas, waiting patiently for more food. The adults and children devoured a pile of delicious ham sandwiches, a huge pork pie, which was Uncle Chris' favourite picnic food, and some cold chicken legs cooked in a sweet brown sauce, with more bags of crisps and lots of fruit juice. What a feast they had. It was strange how William and Lucy were still able to find room for more.

During this second, unexpected picnic tea, Lucy explained to Aunty Liz where they were staying. She pointed in the direction of Rose Cottage Farm and told told her about the Grundys, a little bit about Mr Fudge, but nothing about Benjamin and all their other friends in the woods.

Aunty Lizzy sat on the rug, fascinated by what she was hearing and suggested that before their holiday ended they should all come and visit Rose Cottage Farm. She would dearly love to meet the Grundys and she wanted to introduce Thomas and Katie to the silent Mr Fudge. If that was alright with William and Lucy of course?

"It would be lovely," said Lucy. William wasn't so sure, but didn't say anything in case he upset the picnic atmosphere that he was enjoying so much. He thought to himself, would the Grundys mind if his cousins turned up at the farm unannounced? Would Mr Fudge react if too many humans suddenly came to the potato field to meet him? Might he just pretend not to notice them? That could upset his other country friends and would certainly upset him and his sister.

At last the picnic was over. Happy seemed to have eaten his fill and was snoring and grunting quietly on the rug beside the empty plates, no doubt dreaming of supper and what Thomas was going to give him later that evening. Its funny how small dragons don't really lie down; they just squat on their bottoms and snooze. With everyone helping, it took no time to clear up the empties, pack the hamper and stow it in the sailing boat.

Before their cousins left them to sail off to their holiday home on the other side of the lake, William gave them the directions to find Rose Cottage farm from the main road.

"Don't forget it's a narrow road Uncle Chris and you can't drive fast down it," he said, looking uneasily at Aunty Liz, who did most of the driving on holiday anyway. He knew what she was like sometimes. He also suggested that as there was no telephone at the farm to warn the Grundys about their visit, they should try to visit next Saturday in the early afternoon.

He would have to warn Mr and Mrs Grundy, but deep down he knew they wouldn't mind. Mrs Grundy would put on a special farm tea, including something special for Happy if he was allowed to come with them. That was up to Tom to decide.

It was time for the family to scramble into the sailing boat and settle down on the wooden seats. "Come on you lot," called Uncle Chris, who was in charge. He pulled on the ropes and raised the two small sails. Thomas pulled up the dripping anchor, getting water all over the boat. They waved goodbye and sailed off to the other side of the lake to collect their car and make for their holiday home.

As a watery, pale orange sun started to settle in the horizon behind the old tower, it was a very tired William and Lucy who made their way back across the fields to Rose Cottage. Lucy had the picnic rug around her shoulders

With legs aching from all the walking and climbing over gates,
they chatted to each other all the way home

and William carried the hamper, much lighter now than it had been earlier in the day. It had been a super afternoon. They'd seen so much and to meet their cousins was the best surprise anyone could wish for.

Although they were both feeling jolly tired, with legs aching from all the walking and climbing over gates, they chatted to each other all the way home about the forthcoming visit next Saturday, and whether their wildlife friends would be pleased to meet their cousins.

"You know it's a bit of a risk," suggested William, as he changed his grip on the basket . The wicker hamper was beginning to feel heavy and he wished they were back at the farm instead of having Lower Meadow still to cross.

The late afternoon sun had settled behind the far hills and woods as the two struggled to close the yard gate behind them. Taking off their shoes at the back door they nearly fell inside, dropping the rug and hamper on the floor, too tired to put them away. It was naughty but understandable in the circumstances.

Mrs Grundy was baking bread for the next day. They could smell the warm, doughy aroma that filled the kitchen as the fresh bread was baked in the lower oven of the Aga. They plonked themselves down at the kitchen table and with tired arms put the empty basket on the only available spare space on the table.

"That was a lovely picnic Mrs Grundy, thank you very much," said Lucy, resting her weary head on her arms.

Mrs Grundy placed large glasses of fresh juice in front of them and they tried to tell her about the afternoon's adventures and about Thomas' friend

Happy the dragon. They told her how their cousins from London had sailed across the lake, bringing another picnic tea with them. Two teas in one afternoon had filled them so full that they couldn't possibly eat supper this evening.

"That's all right my dears, she said, smiling at them warmly as if she already knew about Happy, but of course she didn't. She just thought it was another of the convincing tales that the two children so good at making up.

"You should write a storybook about all these tales," she said to Lucy as she popped another tin of white dough into the Aga's large oven, taking out one that was cooked and shaking the warm bread on to a wire tray. That was three she had made and enough for the next few days.

William smiled as he looked at Lucy. He knew that someone was already writing about their adventures on the farm, but it was their secret; for now, anyway. One day, he thought to himself, we will have to let the Grundys read them, but not now. There are still a few more adventures to have before the story book is finished.

Tired but happy, the two youngsters sat in front of the warm Aga, enjoying the delicious aroma of baking bread wafting from the oven. They waited patiently for Mr Grundy to return from his weekly trip to town so that they could tell him about their adventures.

Chapter 9

Party At Rose Cottage Farm

Before they knew it, Saturday arrived. The past week had gone by so fast, with lots of jobs to do around the farm and helping Mrs Grundy to bake a delicious assortment of cakes for the weekend. It was a particularly warm day for the time of year.

It was quite usual to have a lot of activity around the farmyard on a Saturday. It was the end of the week's work on the farm and there was always a need to get things prepared for the following week. Mr Grundy had decided to clean his old grey Massey Ferguson tractor. It had picked up an unusual amount of mud, especially under the wheel guards where it seemed to build up in layers, making cleaning a difficult job.

Mr Grundy would have to fill the tractor by hand with diesel fuel from the tank at the back of the Dutch barn, then make sure there was enough air in the tyres. It was a job that he didn't like much but these dirty jobs had to be done before putting the tractor away for the weekend. The last task was to check the engine oil, which he did most days, but this tractor was old and used more oil than it should. Tractors were expensive pieces of equipment and although he knew he should replace it, he was very fond of the 'old girl', so he did his best to keep her going as long as he could.

Also today, he also wanted to tidy up the Dutch barn, which hadn't been done for a few months. He prided himself at being quite good at keeping it reasonably tidy, but recently he had let it slip. He likes a tidy barn so that he can find his tools when he wants them without wondering where he had put them down after the last time they had been used. But like most small farmers, his time was valuable and daylight hours had to be spent working the fields. This meant that jobs like tidying up tended to be put to one side. He wasn't proud of himself when that happened.

William wanted to tell him that he wasn't as tidy as his dad, but thought better of it. No need to upset him today of all days, especially as his cousins were coming for tea. He needed to be on his best behaviour and he knew that that would keep Mr Grundy very happy.

The old farmer was also looking forward to meeting William and Lucy's relatives. He and his wife rarely had visitors and were so pleased when William had mentioned that his Aunty Liz and Uncle Chris would like to come and meet them. He and William would make sure that everywhere looked spick and span around the yard. The dusty floor in the barn was sprinkled with water and brushed. Tools were hung up, bits of string put in a hessian bag, along with an old calendar with farming pictures on each page but that was years out of date. The rubbish was thrown away in the old trailer that was parked behind the barn. It was only used for storing and carting rubbish; a weekly trip to the tip the other side of Bluebell Wood.

Not only was there all this activity on the farm, but the day before there had also been a lot of tidying up in the cottage, although Mrs Grundy was a very careful farmer's wife who always liked her home looking clean and comfortable. This morning was going to be a cooking morning and the kitchen was a hive of activity. Mrs Grundy was in charge but Lucy would do most of the baking and she loved every minute of it.

During their holiday visits to the farm, Mrs Grundy had shown many new recipes to Lucy and she would try out some of them for this afternoon's tea party. If they were successful and everyone liked them, she could tell Mummy, who was always keen to try out new ideas. One of Lucy's wishes was that one day she could be able to cook as well as her mother.

This morning she wore her green striped apron, which came down to below her knees. Her hair had been carefully tied back with an elastic band. The huge old wooden kitchen table was covered in flour and baking tins, and trays of angel cakes were ready for the oven. Pats of homemade butter floated in water in china pots and there were jugs of fresh creamy milk from the dairy farm a few miles away. Two dozen large brown eggs from her own hens were waiting to be used. On the shelf behind them were rows of assorted jars of Mrs Grundy's special jams for filling the scones and sandwiches. This was going to be the best farm tea Lucy had ever seen, made especially for their cousins Tom and Katie. Nor would Lucy forget Uncle Chris and Aunty Liz, who always enjoyed their food, wherever they were.

Looking through the kitchen window, you would have thought there was a competition to see who could bake the best cake. Lucy had decided to make her favourite, a sponge cake filled with raspberry jam and cream . This was how she made her cake:

Ingredients:
4 oz self-raising flour
4 oz caster sugar 4 oz fresh farm butter (could be margarine
if no butter available)
2 fresh brown eggs

Method:
Preheat the oven to 140 degrees.
Stir in all the ingredients until pale and smooth.
Measure out a piece of grease-proof paper that fits the tin.
Spoon the mixture in.
Put cake in oven and set timer for 20 minutes.
When ready leave cake to cool for 20 minutes.
When cooled, slice the cake in half horizontally.
Spread a thick layer of jam on the base about 1cm thick
and replace top. Sieve icing sugar on to top surface.

If only Papo could see this, she thought to herself as she took the cooked cake out of the oven and placed it on the table. Mrs Grundy was most impressed by Lucy's work but said, "Lucy, it might look lovely sitting there on the table, but you know my dear, the proof is in the eating."

Mrs Grundy thought that as the men would be so hungry, she would bake a fruit cake that could be sliced into huge portions to have with their cups of tea. It took most of the morning to prepare the afternoon tea. The cakes looked perfect when they came out of the oven, but how would they taste? That was the question everyone wanted to know.

After finishing the dirty, grimy work in the barn and yard , Mr Grundy sent William indoors to wash and comb his hair, which was always all over the place, and to put on a clean shirt and pair of shoes. He was determined that, for once on this holiday, William would look presentable for his cousin's visit.

Time went quickly, with a hurried lunch, and before they knew it there was the sound of car tyres crunching on the gravel yard.

"They're here!" yelled William, rushing out of the back door so quickly that he nearly fell over. Luckily, Lucy just grabbed him and saved him from falling flat on his face. In doing so she covered the back of his blue jumper with white icing from her hands. "Idiot," she murmured under her breath, so that he couldn't hear her.

"Sorry Sis," he laughed and ran towards the car to greet his cousins.

Doors were opened wide and Thomas and little Katie scrambled out of their seats at the back of the car, quicker than Liz and Chris could get out of theirs in the front, but then, they're much younger and certainly more agile.

There were hugs all round, lots of jumping up and down with excitement as Mr and Mrs Grundy appeared by the back door of their cottage, looking very smart in their best clothes. They welcomed everyone to their home and led them through the back door and into the kitchen, which by now was shining like a new pin. What a transformation from the chaos of the morning.

The Grundys were pleased to have these visitors, especially since they had already knew William and Lucy's parents. Now this visit would complete the family circle. Well, not quite. They still hadn't met the grandparents yet, or Uncle Tim Papo's son who lived in London with Aunty T J, but that was unlikely, as they lived so far away and didn't travel much these days. But who knows, they thought, miracles do happen.

When all the laughter, handshakes and excitement had settled down, Mrs Grundy ushered everyone out of the kitchen, down the narrow hallway and into the front room. The front room in all farm cottages is used only on special occasions like weddings, birthdays and important visits like this one. At her invitation, the two grown-ups slumped down into the soft comfortable chairs and allowed the cushions to wrap themselves around their backs. This is sheer old-fashioned farm comfort, thought Aunty Liz and wished she lived in a home that had rooms like this one.

Uncle Chris explained that they had been driving for quite some time, even though their holiday home was just the other side of the lake. It was a long way round on the main road to the turning for the farm, but William's directions had done the trick. Chris admitted that without them, they would never have found the farm in a hundred years! It was in such an isolated location.

The children sat on the carpets while the adults chatted about their holiday, the farm and the lovely Dorset countryside, which was new to Aunty Liz and Uncle Chris. They were 'townies', but Papo had often said that he thought Aunty Liz would maybe like to live in a village one day, as long as there were things to do and people to talk to.

"Don't get too comfortable, folk," chirped up Mr Grundy grinning all over his face. "There's plenty of time before tea and William and Lucy want to show you round our farm. And I know that they are keen to take you to the potato field where their friend Mr Fudge lives."

He told them about Mr Fudge. "I think you'll like him. I made him about two years ago and if you are especially lucky today, you might just meet some of his wildlife friends, but don't be disappointed if you don't," he said with a wide grin. William often secretly wondered whether Mr Grundy believed their stories about the friends that they had made. It's strange, but to this very day he still has no idea how he got back to the cottage the night of the storm and the accident that nearly cost him his life.

"Can we take Happy with us too?" piped up Thomas, as he walked towards the door holding Katie's hand.

"I suppose you can if Mr Grundy doesn't mind having him walking round the farm," replied Lucy.

"But he hasn't met him yet, has he?" said Mummy, butting in.

"I know he hasn't, but I know Mr Grundy will like him," pleaded Thomas in that voice that no one could refuse, not even his mother.

"Who's this Happy then?" asked Mr Grundy, smiling, thinking it might be a dog or one of Katie's stuffed dolls that she had left in the car.

"He's my friend and he's a real live happy dragon," said Thomas as he opened the back door and walked towards the car to fetch him.

Surprise, surprise! The inside of the car was empty. No movement, no noise, no dragon, absolutely nothing.

"He's gone!" shouted Thomas at the top of his voice, which was never

"Who's this 'Happy' then?"

loud at the best of times. "He must have got out when we all did and now I don't know where he is." Suddenly Tom had that look on his face that could very easily turn to tears if nothing was done quickly.

Just at that moment Lucy came out of the cottage putting on her coat. "What's the matter Thomas?" she said, running up to her distraught cousin.

"Happy's disappeared. He got out of the car," he shouted to her. "I can't find him anywhere Lucy. He's gone and I'll never find him, will I?"

"Don't worry Tom, I bet I know where he is," she said, putting an arm round his shoulder to comfort him. "Follow me Tom. Come on everyone, this way. I bet he's gone to look for our friends in the potato field and to meet Mr Fudge. Don't worry Tom, we'll find him soon, I know we will, trust me."

As she hurried to the yard gate Lucy shouted, "Let's go and look for him everyone. If we're lucky we'll also meet our friends and on the way home I want to show you the old tree stump in Bluebell Woods where we sometimes play."

"Will we need our welly boots if we're going to cross those fields?" asked Uncle Chris. He wasn't used to muddy fields, living as he did in London. When it rained, wet pavements were the worst hazards for London dwellers.

"No, it's nearly all grass," explained Mr Grundy reassuringly, "and you will find it very dry in the wood this time of year, so don't worry about putting your boots on, your shoes will be just fine in this weather. Mind you, they will need cleaning when we get back." He put his coat on and hurried to join the others who were already making for the yard gate.

Aunty Liz was not quite so sure about all of this. She hated to get her shoes muddy. Like Uncle Chris, she was happier being a 'townie', although she wouldn't admit that to anyone, especially the younger ones. They all thought she would be up for anything, which was true. She smiled, not wanting to be a nuisance to anyone. She's like that, thought William, that's why we love her so much.

"Off you go, all of you," called out Mrs Grundy. "When you get back, tea will be ready, so don't be too long, no more than an hour at the most." She ushered the stragglers out of the cottage and into the yard.

"This way, come on everyone, follow us." Lucy and William led the group through the yard gate, turned left and started to walk towards the potato field where they hoped to meet Fudge and some of his friends.

"Can you see over there?" shouted William, pointing slightly to the right as they crossed Lower Meadow. "Up there, along the top of the grass bank that's peppered with rabbit holes. That's the hedge which Mr Grundy was laying last year when the storm caused all that damage and nearly killed him."

112

They looked over to their right where he was pointing and saw the neatly laid hedge with its branches and thick stems leaning in one direction. It looked quite unreal from that distance. Along its length, new green shoots were appearing that gave it a pale green sheen between the angled brown branches of the hedge.

"That's lovely," commented Aunty Liz, pointing it out to Thomas and Katie. Mr Grundy grinned behind his shaggy beard. He was very pleased that William had pointed out the hedge and that they liked it so much. As he walked along behind the main group he thought to himself, I must remember that it's a nice feeling to receive praise from other people if you've done something well. I will have to praise Mrs Grundy and the children more when they do something well. He smiled to himself and followed on, lost in his own thoughts.

Lucy pointed out the rooks' nests in two of the old oak trees on the right of the hedge at the top of the field. "Do you know," she explained, "they come back every year and when their young chicks hatch, the adults feed them on the new potatoes. That's why Mr Grundy made Mr Fudge and that's why he guards them day and night."

"That seems logical to me," Uncle Chris thought to himself, but then how could a dummy scarecrow keep the rooks away?

Katie was holding on to Lucy's hand and trying to walk faster than everyone else. She wasn't really interested in hedges and things like that. She just wanted to meet Mr Fudge and his friends. She had heard so many tales about him from her cousins but didn't think he really existed.

The group crossed Lower Meadow without getting too muddy and arrived at the field gate, which to their surprise was open. There, in the middle of the field and with his arms wide outstretched was Mr Fudge, resplendent in his black top hat and tatty old raincoat. Chris now realised why he scared the rooks. Looking at him even sent a slight shiver down his spine. Was this really the Mr Fudge that they had all heard so much about?

Then, to their great surprise, they saw Happy sitting close to Mr Fudge, staring up at his turnip face. Lucy had been right all along, clever old thing.

"Quiet everyone, please don't move a muscle," said Lucy, letting go of Katie's hand. "I think that they are talking to each other and I want to hear what they are saying." Nobody moved as she listened.

"I can't hear a word, Lucy," whispered Thomas.

"Nor can I," said Aunty Liz looking a bit perplexed.

"Of course you can't," explained Lucy, "Only William and I have been taught how to understand his language. Please be quiet everyone," she said again, quietly but more firmly this time.

"I wish I could understand them. What are they saying?" asked Uncle Chris, who was now holding Katie in his arms to keep her quiet. They looked at Happy, knowing that something must be up because he was shaking his head and flapping his tiny wings with excitement as he looked up into the scarecrow's turnip face.

Mr Fudge suddenly saw the group of humans by the gate. He didn't recognise some of them and thinking they were strangers, he stopped talking to Happy. The dragon turned and saw Tom standing in the gateway. He flapped his wings and jumped up into the air, waddling towards his friend, obviously very pleased to see him.

Mr Fudge was very relieved that Happy knew Tom, but he still felt apprehensive about the other humans in the group. But he didn't say a word, not even to William or Lucy as he stood motionless with outstretched arms.

Mr Grundy couldn't believe what he was seeing. He took off his glasses and rubbed his eyes with a red hanky. "What's all this about then?" he exclaimed at the sight of Tom and the little red dragon. So it was true after all. Young Tom really did have a pet dragon! Dear Mrs Grundy would never believe him if he hadn't seen it with his own eyes.

There was no movement from Mr Fudge, not even a hint that he recognised his dear friends, but William and Lucy understood that it was not the right time to let Mr Grundy into their secret. There will be time for that later. However, they were both thrilled that their cousins had met Mr Fudge and had seen what a great fellow he was. Mr Grundy had done a splendid job, making a scarecrow look so lifelike. They decided to leave the scarecrow in peace to continue doing what he is so good at doing, scaring away the rooks.

The afternoon had flashed by without anyone noticing the time and it was now too late to visit Bluebell Wood. The grown-ups wanted to get back to the farm for a cup of tea and a taste of those freshly baked cakes. Who was going to win the competition, Lucy's sponge cake or Mrs Grundy's fruit cake?

At this time of the year, the end of each day comes quickly to a close. Evenings rapidly turn to night and Aunty Liz had to drive them to the holiday farm, down the narrow lanes.

They said their 'Thank Yous' and 'Goodbyes' and promised to visit the farm again at the Grundys' invitation. It had been such a happy occasion and everyone had got on well. Tom wished he could have stayed longer but Katie was tired after all the excitement and just wanted to get home to her bed.

Chapter 10

Things Mechanical

There was nothing William liked more than pulling on his dirty old greasy trousers, slipping into his black jumper, which was really blue when it was clean, and helping Mr Grundy in the farm workshop. He loved all the different workshop tools and gadgets that lay around everywhere, underneath and on top of the dusty wooden work benches.

As he watched William at the bench, Mr Grundy thought that the boy would make a good engineer when he grows up. He had learned many new skills and was jolly good at putting things together with his hands. Of course, even if he didn't become an engineer, being practical and handy is important in life, he thought to himself. On the other hand, William might want to be a pilot like his dad.

The old man was also impressed that, for one so young, William could follow the instruction in a manual when he had something to build, like a model helicopter or toy car. Not bad for a boy of his age, he thought as he watched him mucking around on the bench with some of his special tools, the ones that he normally used on his tractor.

The thought came into his head that it might be time to show him the old machinery parts hidden deep inside Bluebell Wood. They were near the derelict quarry and had been there for as long as he could remember. There wasn't really much to show him, but he thought that William might be interested, just as he had been when he first found them when he was William's age.

Mr Grundy had no idea what they were or where they came from but he thought that if he and William could get them out next holiday, he might find it interesting to have a go at cleaning them. It will give him something interesting to do, he thought, instead of following me around the farm doing odd jobs.

That evening after tea when they had tidied up and put away the dishes, they gathered in the front sitting room, which was a real treat for the children.

When they were all comfortable, Mr Grundy told them about the pile of old, rusty machinery in Bluebell Wood, now completely covered in weeds and brambles. He told them how he had first found them years ago when he was a small boy, about William's age.

"In those days the farm was much bigger than it is to day. We milked the cows by hand and my father worked the farm with a team of farm labourers, that's what we called them in those days," he said. "They did all the hard work, so as a young boy I had plenty of time to go exploring all over the farm. Sometimes to places that I shouldn't have gone to."

William and Lucy were fascinated. Dear old Mrs Grundy stopped her knitting and listened, because even after all these years being married to this lovely man and living on this very farm, she had never heard this story before. She thought, I wonder if he is making it up just to tease the children! Getting his own back for all the stories they keep telling him.

Speaking quite softly, he continued with his tale, which now took a different tack. "As long ago as I can remember, I was told that there was a very old sea chest up in the attic. My dad told me it was far too heavy for him to lift, so it's been up there all my life. I think it was there even before my father was a boy. I have seen it once or twice, but it's at the far end of the roof, right under the eaves and difficult to get at. Now then, if I remember rightly, it's covered in a tatty old black blanket, full of holes.

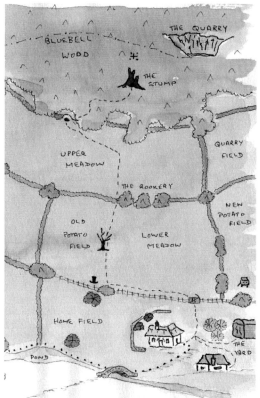

"I bet those holes have been made by generations of field mice, friends of Mr Fudge, that have lived up there under the warm straw roof," said Lucy, who had been listening intently to his story and was now very interested in the thought of an old sea chest, right above their heads in the attic.

Looking at the two children over his glasses and knowing that he had their total attention, he continued with his story. "Remember when we first met you that summer, Lucy? When you arrived at the farm in your dad's big red Volvo? You told me about the scroll in the bottle that you and William and your Papo had found in the cave near Lyme Regis. Do you remember?"

"Yes, I do remember it very clearly," said Lucy, thinking back to that happy and eventful day when the family first visited Rose Cottage Farm.

"Well you two, since then I've given it a lot of thought and I believe that I have the answer to the riddle. You know, the riddle that you found in the bottle.

"Have you?" they asked together excitedly.

"I am sure the answer to that riddle is in our attic chest and we must get that chest opened as soon as possible if we are to solve this mystery," he said triumphantly. "I believe the riddle was telling us to look in the chest for something special. Maybe there's a clue in it, or several clues, or maybe even a very special object."

"It could be valuable and worth a lot of money," said William, shaking with excitement and nearly falling out of his chair.

"Go on please," said Lucy, wanting to know more but trying hard to be grown up and not show how excited she was. Mr Grundy continued with his story.

"About fifteen years ago I went up into the attic to look for some old maps of the farm that I thought were stored in a box up there. You see, there was a boundary dispute with one of my neighbours, not a serious one mind you, but I needed to find out where some field boundaries existed in the old days, before my father was even born, in fact. Down near the water meadows, by the lake, there are some medieval hedges, or what's left of them. They were planted over four hundred years ago and my neighbour and I weren't sure if they were the real boundary or not. His modern maps didn't show them and we needed to find out the facts, so it wasn't a really serious dispute.

"While I was up in the attic rummaging around, I found the sea chest that my father had told me about all those years before. It was still covered by a tatty old rug.

"I pulled the rug off carefully so as not to make too much dust, I tried to open the lid but it was fastened with a huge padlock. I couldn't budge it. I even tried to pull the chest towards the hatch with the idea of getting it down, but the eaves of the thatched roof are so low there, I couldn't stand up, so I just left it there and covered it up again. I forgot all about it until you two came along with your story, and that made me think about it again."

"Did you find the old farm maps?" William asked, looking intently into Mr Grundy's wrinkled face.

"No William, I didn't find them. I had a long chat about it and eventually agreed with my neighbour where the boundary should be and he arranged to have some new maps printed. I have them in the kitchen drawer by the back door.

"Now you two, I have been thinking very seriously about recent events," he continued. "Do you think the mermaid in the cave was a ghostly figure that appears when someone enters the cave? She appears, hoping that they will find the glass bottle, because she wants them to then pick it up and read the writing on the scroll. I know you told me that if there's a noise she disappears, as does the sea chest. But the bottle remained and you have it, don't you?"

They were fascinated by his idea. "Do go on please Mr Grundy," said Lucy. "What else do you think?"

"I believe you only thought you saw a mermaid and the chest, but they were not really there, it was just your imagination. I believe that someone wants you to find the bottle and they created the mermaid image to help you find it."

"Wow, do you really believe that?" asked William, who ever since he was a young boy was fascinated by strange stories and the supernatural.

It seemed to Lucy to be a fantastic idea and the excitement sent a shiver down her back. But thinking back to that day in the cave and how real the mermaid had seemed to the three of them, she had doubts about Mr Grundy's theory. On the other hand, the mermaid and the chest had vanished when William cried out to warn them about the incoming tide. It was also true that Papo did bring the old bottle out of the cave and she knew he didn't have it with him when they went in.

So there must be some truth in it somewhere, but where? And anyway Papo had no idea that Rose Cottage ever existed. She just knew that Papo wouldn't play tricks on them like that. Anyway, where would he have found such an old glass bottle in the first place? No, she thought, it wasn't Papo, this time.

After a slight hesitation while she collected her thoughts, she said, "You could be right you know, but on the other hand, unless we open the chest we'll never know, will we?"

"Why don't we open the chest tomorrow?" said a quiet voice behind them. Mrs Grundy had put her knitting on the table. "If you want to know the answer to that riddle, we must all try and solve it together," she said smiling at the three of them.

"In the meantime, who would like a mug of hot chocolate before we go to bed? You two need to be fit and ready for tomorrow. I think we are all going to have a very busy day. First in the attic and then if there's time, in Bluebell Wood."

Was it that late? How had the evening gone so quickly with no one noticing the old clock in the hall chiming the hours away? It was after eleven o'clock and on holiday they would normally be tucked up in bed by nine.

With mugs of hot chocolate in their hands, they said good night to the Grundys, quietly shut the cottage back door behind them and walked across the yard towards their room, helped by the light of a bright moon. The small holiday house had been their 'home from home' ever since they arrived at Rose Cottage nearly three years ago. For William and Lucy it seemed a lifetime since that summer afternoon at the caravan site, searching the maps for clues to answer the riddle they'd found in the old glass bottle. How excited they had been when Lucy found the farm in one of her map squares and the family followed the map to discover the farm and the Grundys.

So much had happened to them since then. There had been loads of exciting times here at the farm and also happy times at home and school. Grandma Ruthy and Papo T had sold Church House and were hoping to live in a slightly smaller home next door to Beech House to be close to their family in Kineton. The grandchildren were both enjoying school and all the activities associated with it. William was playing lots of sport, particularly rugger, and Lucy was enjoying the upper school.

She was a tall girl. What pleased Papo and Mamo so much about Lucy was that she had started to learn how to play the piano. Mamo sometimes made them all laugh when she tinkled with the keys and pretended to play. Papo, so we were told, when he was a young boy a little older than Lucy is now, had years and years of lessons but now couldn't play a note, which was a shame because playing the piano when you're older gives you so much pleasure, and of course, pleasure to other people.

Besides all these activities since coming to the cottage that summer, William and Lucy had met and become very friendly with the Little People. Benjamin had showed them more fascinating country scenes and Mr Fudge was at last given a new 'old coat', as the original old one had been completely eaten away by the field mice that lived in his pockets. There were so many mice enjoying his company that many now lived in his other pockets too. However, what pleased Mr Fudge more than anything

was in his top pocket. Living there in a ball of straw and dried grass was a dormouse. He had become quite tame and Lucy would often lift him gently out of Fudge's pocket and hold him between her thumb and finger. His lovely round dark brown eyes twinkled in the daylight and his saucer-shaped ears twitched continuously, as did his whiskers.

Was this summer visit to the farm going to be the beginning of yet another exciting adventure for the two of them? Lucy thought that it just had to be, now that they had Mr Grundy to help them solve the riddle of the sea chest .

It was late and they were both jolly tired as they jumped into a hot bath, which eased the aches in their muscles. Lucy went first, while William sat on his bunk bed, his mind wandering into Bluebell Wood and to thoughts of the hidden machinery that Mr Grundy had told them about that evening. I wonder what they are, how big they are, and I wonder what they're from? he mused. Then Lucy called out, "Bath ready William," and that jolted him back to the here and now.

Unusually, William had a restless night, tossing this way and that so that his duvet ended up on the floor and he slept with no covers on. He was restless, not because he was worried about anything in particular, nor because he thought he was back at school with exams coming up soon. That didn't really worry him. It was just that his mind was occupied with all that Mr Grundy had told them.

He woke early and very cold with the sun streaming through the window onto his bed. Lucy hadn't stirred during the night. Waking early wasn't usual for William because he liked his bed and always got up after Lucy when they were on holiday. But today was different, thanks to that duvet!

They dressed quickly in their holiday clothes, made their bunk beds, put away yesterday's dirty clothes in the large wicker basket, tidied the room and raced across the yard to the cottage for breakfast. This was going to be a special day and William wanted to eat his breakfast quickly.

"William dear, don't gobble down your food like a fat turkey," said Mrs Grundy, smiling at him affectionately as she buttered some pure white bread with homemade butter and jam. "There's plenty of time to finish your bacon and egg. And Lucy, try to eat some of the egg white dear, you know it's good for you."

"You know I don't like the white bit," retorted Lucy with her mouth full of bread. She loved the fresh bread more than the warm toast which was always thickly spread with strawberry jam.

"I made that toast especially for you this morning. You'll both need plenty of good food inside you if you and Mr Grundy hope to find out about all that machinery in Bluebell Wood," she said encouragingly. "But before that, you

both need to get up into our attic. Try to open that old chest and see what's inside," she said, smiling as she fussed about the breakfast table putting out clean cutlery and plates for her husband who was out on the tractor.

The two finished their breakfast with gusto, not saying a word to each other or to Mrs Grundy, who was busy washing some dirty plates in the sink.

"Mr Grundy's not here at the moment," she said. "He had to go to the garage on the main road, you know, that one near the cross roads. He's gone to get some more diesel for the tractor, William. He told me it's nearly run out after all that work you did yesterday."

William couldn't settle down to anything after breakfast. He fidgeted like a cat on a hot tin roof. So, to keep himself occupied and out of mischief he walked around the yard at least three times, inspected the tractor in the barn and then walked over the stone bridge and along the hard farm track, where he met Mr Grundy on his way home.

After his breakfast, which is an important meal of the day for farmers, everyone sat around the kitchen table waiting expectantly for Mr Grundy to explain how he thought they should organise the day.

"We need to get up into the roof space and open the chest first," he explained as he drank his hot tea. "Then," and he paused, "once we have found out what's inside the chest, we can all sit down again and decide what to do next." Everyone, even Mrs Grundy, thought that was a very good idea indeed. At last breakfast was over and they were ready to start exploring the attic. Mr Grundy gave them their first orders of the day.

"William, will you please go and get the set of steps from the Dutch barn. Lucy, will you go and help him, as it will need two of you to carry it across the yard and into the house."

They scampered off in the direction of the barn and Mr Grundy turned to his wife, smiling, "My dear, I really do think that there's a mystery up in our attic in that old sea chest. And with the help of the children I mean to find out about it one way or the other." He chuckled confidently to himself, "You know, the more I think about that scroll, the more I am sure about my ideas and I

William walked around the yard at least three times and then walked over the stone bridge and along the hard farm track

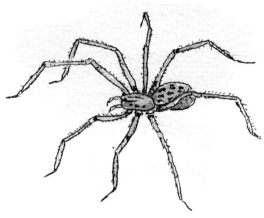

really do mean to find out what it's all about. Luckily we have the children here to help."

A few minutes later they were back, puffing and out of breath, carrying the folding steps between them. The steps were just long enough to reach the loft hatch from the hallway. Lucy pleaded to go first, so the 'men' gave in and let her, as usual!

"You'll need a torch. In fact you might need two," said Mrs Grundy, looking for them in the kitchen cupboard under the draining board. She had replaced both with new batteries last week so they should give plenty of light for the morning's activities.

"You hold the steps firmly William," directed Mr Grundy, "in case they are a bit wobbly when Lucy climbs up. Then you go up next and I'll hold the steps for you. Then Mrs Grundy can hold the steps for me and pass up the two torches when I'm up there. It will be very dark under that old thatch."

The attic space in the old cottage had not been disturbed for many years, except by the families of house mice and the hundreds of spiders that made their home in the dry straw thatch.

Lucy slid the hatch door to one side as she climbed up and the others quickly followed, hauling themselves up into the attic from the steps to sit on the boards that had been nailed around the hatch opening. The still air had an old, fusty smell about it, a mixture of mice droppings and decay. Everywhere was covered in a thick layer of grey dust.

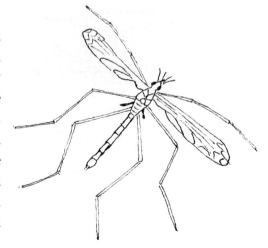

The unpleasant smell stuck in their throats but it didn't stop them from crawling slowly along a narrow strip of boards that covered the ancient beams in the centre of the roof, leading to the far gable end. William thought it was lucky that they had the two torches to show them the way in the gloom, otherwise anything could have happened, even falling through the ceiling if they slipped off the boards.

They had to be very careful as they inched their way on hands and knees along the boards. The trick was to make sure that they didn't get their heads caught up in the huge cobwebs hanging from the roof, or the bits of long hanging straw. A slight slip and they might fall through the ceiling into the downstairs room. That would be a disaster, thought Lucy as she edged her way towards the far wall.

Leading the way, she was the first to see the pile of old clothes and the tatty old rug that partially covered the sea chest in the corner under the low straw eaves. It looked a little bigger than the one she remembered in the cave, but in the beam of her torch the shape and colour looked the same, as far as she could tell.

Crawling carefully behind her with the second torch, came William. Already he looked like something from outer space, grubby, hair all over the place and difficult to distinguish him from the pile of old clothes in the corner. Boys will be boys, thought his older sister as she looked at him.

"Wow! Look at that. Do you think it's the same sea chest we saw in the cave Lucy?"

"Could be," she said, spitting dust out of her mouth as Mr Grundy came towards them on his hands and knees, awkwardly pulling a length of rope behind him that they would need to move the chest.

"If it isn't the very same one, it certainly looks like it," she said. Then, correcting herself, she added, "It can't be the same one, because the other one in the cave was an apparition. So this must be the real one." Even though it was hot under this straw roof she began to shiver slightly with anticipation. Turning to the others she said, "Let's try pulling it into the middle of the attic quickly, because this horrible smell is making me feel sick." She began to cough and splutter.

"I'll do it Sis," Said William, taking an end of the rope from Mr Grundy and crawling carefully past Lucy. Stretching out, he tied the end around one of the iron handles that was poking out from under the rug. With the other hand he gently pulled off the old rug, immediately disturbing a cloud of dust and loads of creepy crawlies, which scampered off into the dark of the roof space. He didn't mind because he was used to playing with insects of all shapes and sizes, but he knew that Lucy hated them.

It took the three of them several more minutes of hard and careful pulling in the hot, dusty atmosphere. They heaved this way and that, slowly easing the chest from under the eaves. Eventually they managed to pull it on to the boards in the middle of the attic. Luckily, whoever had put the chest there in the first place had left it on a scrap of wood which made it slightly easier to drag towards the centre of the roof.

Poor William, what did he look like, covered in dust and muck, with cobwebs covering his head and hair? But his face was a picture of success with a smile from one ear to the other. He didn't mind getting dirty, he loved it. I've done it! he thought, and now we can get it open.

With the chest resting on the narrow boards in the centre of the roof, they had more light from the two torches, but they needed to get their breath back and the dust out of their mouths. Mr Grundy called down to his wife to ask for some glasses of cold water, which soon appeared. Wiping their filthy faces with dirty hankies, they gulped down the refreshing liquid, which washed away the dust taste in their mouths. But the smell of mice still lingered on their clothes and hair.

While the others watched, Mr Grundy produced a large metal crowbar that he had brought from the workshop. He slipped the pointed end between the rusty lock and the chest and brought all his weight down on the free end. There was a sudden crack, like a pistol shot, as the rusty lock gave way under his massive heave.

"Well done!" choked William, looking at the broken lock lying on the boards. Although made of some sort of metal, it had shattered as it fell fell on to the boards with a thump, raising yet more dust. They knew that soon the chest would give up its secrets. After all these years, thought William, all would be revealed! But the thought sent another chill down Lucy's spine.

As she was the only girl, Mr Grundy and William let Lucy have the honour of opening the wooden lid. They shone their torches on to the sea chest. Trembling with excitement, Lucy

The rusty lock gave way

carefully placed her fingers under the lid and lifted. To her amazement it moved without much effort. After two hundred years here in the attic, its hinges still worked and she pushed the lid back as far as it would go. Now, in the light of the two torches and with bated breath, they peered into the chest. Would it be full of treasure?

Half way down in the chest and neatly laid out were what looked like some old, faded sea clothes. Lucy reached in and gently lifted out a faded dark blue coat from the top of the pile. Holding it carefully, she saw there were two old, tarnished, gold epaulettes attached to the shoulders. The cuffs were beautifully finished with faded gold lace. The jacket had wide blue lapels reaching down to the waist, with gold lace round the edges and black buttons down the centre. Underneath the blue jacket lay a pair of faded white breeches, yellowed with age, and a beautifully embroided waistcoat.

"These things must have belonged to someone very important," she said.

Before they took out any more of the clothing, Mr Grundy called down to his wife, asking her to hand up a large table cloth. He realized that the clothes were too precious to put on to the dusty boards.

Delving deeper into the chest, Lucy found that underneath the clothes was a pair of black leather shoes, each with its own buckle. Lying alongside, wrapped in what looked like sailcloth, was a sword in a black scabbard. Next to the sword was a faded black cocked hat, still with its yellowy gold tassels attached and gold wire threaded along its edges.

"These are so beautiful," said Lucy, as she ran her hands over the faded clothing and lightly touched the sword scabbard. As he looked at the clothes, William recognised that they must have once belonged to a senior ship's captain. He had seen similar uniforms in naval war books that Papo had shown him and he knew that English naval officers wore these things two or three

hundred years ago. Gently easing the hat and sword to one side, Lucy found a well-worn black eye patch.

They placed the clothes carefully in the tablecloth and passed them downstairs to Mrs Grundy, before William returned to exploring the chest. To one side and hidden from view there was a large square mahogany box, wedged into place with rolled balls of sailcloth, similar to the material used to wrap the sword. The box had no lock and clasp, but it did look rather heavy.

"You lift it out please William," said Mr Grundy, and he and Lucy shone their torches on to the wooden box. William lifted it out carefully and laid it on the floor boards next to the sea chest. As he removed the casket, William saw that underneath were sheets of yellowed paper that he thought might be maps. He lifted them up to catch the light of the torches. They were maps, but not maps of the sea, as they would have expected, but maps of the land.

Seeing them, Mr Grundy said, "William, would you please look after the mahogany box and get it downstairs? We can open it on the kitchen table where there's more light and we can see what we're doing. Lucy dear, could you please carry down these old maps? Be careful as you go down the ladder. We'll spread them out on the kitchen table after we've looked inside the box."

"Before I leave the attic I'm just going to have another look round in case there's something else we've missed," said Mr Grundy. "Then I'll close the chest for the time being because I think we've got out what's really important to us. We can come back later to collect the other things when we've looked at the box and the old maps."

With the mahogany box under one arm, William crawled back to the hatch opening. Lucy managed more easily as the old maps were much lighter as she moved backwards on her hands and knees.

The three very dirty and dishevelled people stood happily in the middle of the kitchen admiring the beautiful square mahogany box, which Mrs Grundy had now wiped with a damp cloth. The faded maps were placed on the table and a very surprised Mrs Grundy looked at the hoard, especially admiring the pile of old naval clothing now unwrapped from the tablecloth.

"What have we got here?" she asked in surprise, as she led a grubby-faced William and Lucy to the sink to wipe their hands and face with a damp towel. It smudged the dirt and made a grey mess all over their faces. Clapping her hands she said, "Before we do anything else, I think all three of you should go and wash and change your clothes and before lunch we'll all look at these wonderful things you've brought down from our attic."

No one was going to argue with Mrs Grundy when she was in this mood, not even her husband. She was just a little like Mamo in that sense. She wanted the children always to look clean and presentable, not like a couple of urchins.

Instead of just washing their hands and faces, which were now streaked and grubby, it was easier for Lucy and William to jump into a hot soapy bath, so that they could wash out all the dirt and grimy cobwebs from their hair, ears and eyes. They piled their filthy clothes in a heap in the corner with other clothes that needed washing.

"I feel much better now," said William, smiling angelically as he and Lucy returned to the kitchen with scrubbed faces, clean and combed hair and fresh clothes. They were even more eager now to look inside the mahogany box for hidden treasures!

"PLEASE, let's look inside the box first, let's find out what's inside it," pleaded Lucy in the voice that normally helped her to get her own way.

For once, to her surprise, Mr Grundy agreed. "OK then, and after the box, I think we should examine the maps to see what they tell us, hopefully something interesting," he said as his wife and the two children, waiting with glorious anticipation of finding something exciting in the box.

The mahogany box was black and rather grimy, even after Mrs Grundy's attempts to give it a quick clean.But it was well-made and had probably been a beautiful object when new.

Mrs Grundy said she thought that once upon a time it must have been an important ornament for someone rather special.

"I once saw a box, similar to this one, in a museum in Lyme Regis," she said, "but that was when I was a young girl and I lived there with my parents. If I remember correctly, there was a sign identifying the box in the glass show case." No one spoke for a few seconds waiting patiently for her to say something else.

"What did the sign say dear?" asked her husband lovingly.

"I think," she said hesitantly, "it said, 'Common Seafarer's writing box with hidden latch'."

"This must be just like the one you saw in the museum," said Lucy excitedly, "because it's tightly closed and I can't see a lock for the lid." They could see that quite clearly as they looked round the four sides. It was

Common seafarer's writing box

certainly firmly shut and there was no lock or clasp keeping it closed.

"How are we going to solve this puzzle then?" asked William, getting a bit frustrated with everything that was going on. He wanted some action and all they were doing was talking. What he wanted was to get back into the loft and get that sword down. That would be more fun than an old wooden box which no one could open.

They each examined the box for clues, turning it this way and that, without any luck. Then Lucy suddenly piped up.

"You know William, Papo has a small wooded box that our great granny used to own. It's on his dressing table and that's a secret one too. He showed me once how it worked. You have to hold the box in one hand then slide the front of the box along with your fingers of the other hand, and that unlocks the lid. It's simple really."

They watched as she bent over the box again and with some firm pressure tried to move the front of the box. First to the left, then to the right and on her second attempt, the whole front panel started to move to the left.

"We've done it!" shouted William now showing renewed interest in the box.

"You mean your sister has done it," corrected Mrs Grundy.

Lucy hesitated. She knew they had cracked the puzzle and could now open the box.

"You do it Mrs Grundy, you open it for us and we'll just watch," said Lucy, beaming her wide grin for all to see.

"My word Lucy, do you mean that?" she asked, smiling with the familiar look that the children loved to see when she was happy. She was obviously excited at the thought of opening this treasure box. Very carefully, her plump fingers opened the lid. It was stiff after all the years in the chest and it creaked a bit on its two hidden brass hinges, but she managed to do it without too much difficulty.

"There," she said, "it's done," and they all peered inside to see what the box had hidden inside it. The look on their faces told it all: disappointment. There were no precious gleaming gems, no dazzling gold bracelets, no diamonds sparkling up at them. Just two pieces of old sackcloth, stained with age, folded at the bottom of the box. But something hard wrapped in each piece of folded cloth.

William picked out one of the little parcels, carefully laying it on the table, and slowly and gently unwrapped it. Within the folds of the cloth was a small metal object about six inches long that looked like a key and a large piece of folded yellow parchment. Spreading it out on the table, they could just make out a crudely-drawn picture. At first glance it looked like a piece of machinery. There were two smaller, faded drawings on similar parchment attached to the back of the larger sheet.

Picking out the other folded cloth, Lucy unwrapped it to reveal a tarnished gold ring.

"Treasure at last," she murmured and they looked in amazement at the beautiful object. It wasn't an ordinary ring like the ones that Mummy or Grandma Ruthie wore on special occasions. This ring was larger than theirs and it had an emblem engraved on it. Lucy couldn't quite make out what it was.

"Just a minute Lucy dear." Mr Grundy went to one of the kitchen drawers and picked out his large hand-held magnifying glass. Giving it to Lucy he asked her to look closer at the emblem and to tell them what she could see.

"I'm not very sure," she said, "I think it's a dragon, maybe not, or something that looks like a dragon," she explained to them. Then, "Yes, it is, it's a dragon with small wings and some writing underneath it."

This is fascinating, thought William, a real gold ring with a dragon on it. What could it possibly mean? Who once owned this beautiful ring? If it was the sailor who owned the clothes in the chest, then who was he and was he very important? Was he a hero from long ago? William had a most fertile mind when it came to mysteries and the longer they stayed at the farm, more and more puzzles kept on cropping up. Would they ever be able to find out all the answers? Here was yet another riddle to add to all the others.

Once all the excitement and chatter had settled down William turned to the drawings, turning them this way and that, in fact all ways. After pondering for a while, he announced to everyone that he thought, only thought mind you, he knew what they might be.

"These drawings are like the building instructions I get when Daddy buys me a model to make. But these are very old and complicated and I can't read the writing on the sheets. I can't even guess what the machine is. It's not like one I have ever seen before," he said, a little disappointed. Lucy looked over his shoulder and pointed to the date in the bottom corner of the bigger sheet. It read '1750' in very strange flowery lettering.

"Gosh, that's over 250 years ago," she said in amazement. "No wonder you can't read the writing William, it's in old English and even I can't read that."

"So it is," he said, the others wondering what it was all about. Here they had drawings of some sort of machine, a metal object that looked like a key, and a large gold ring engraved with a dragon emblem. It was all very baffling.

"I think we'll need to get some help with these," suggested Mr Grundy, as he looked again at the old drawings and turned the ring over and over in the palm of his hand.

With the drawings now spread out on the table, William hadn't said a word for over ten minutes, possibly longer. The others were wondering what he was thinking because being quiet was not one of William's virtues. He looked at the drawings intently and mumbled to himself, which he does when he is deep in thought and is trying to find an answer to a difficult problem.

The others were a little bit disappointed at the contents of the box, but thrilled with the ring. Lucy had hoped for more excitement when they first saw the box, maybe some wonderful treasure stored all these years inside it. However, she thought, there were still the naval clothes and the sword, which she knew William would love to have hanging on his bedroom wall at home.

She went to the cupboard to fetch a glass for some juice and turning to the others said, "You know, all this must have a purpose, otherwise, why did someone put the plans and the ring in this box in the first place?"

"That's true," said Mr Grundy, also thinking what it could all be about.

Mrs Grundy was totally perplexed but offered the suggestion that Mr Fudge would look grand in the blue uniform.

"What?" replied William in horror. "Put this uniform on Fudge? You can't do that, it's far too valuable Mrs Grundy. We must keep it safe. You never know, it could be worth a lot money one day."

They ate a rather sombre lunch, without much chatter, which was unusual because normally everyone talked at once when they were in the kitchen. However, each in their own way, they were thinking about what they had discovered in the chest and box. After the plates had been cleared away, Mr Grundy replaced the ring in its folded cloth along with the small pieces of parchment and put them back in the box, which he placed on the sideboard. There was a lot of thinking to be done on this one, he mused.

With the table cleared of clutter, he once again spread out some of the larger land maps that they had found in the bottom of the sea chest. He was interested to know more about them and what they might convey, if anything.

"Let's spend some time and see what we can find here," he said, more in hope than expectation, as they all stood round the table staring at the faded maps. The lines, the unintelligible writing and strange drawings and images which must mean something. If only they knew. In fact, it didn't take him long to recognise what he was looking at.

"Look at this," he said excitedly, pointing his finger at a spot on the map. "I'm sure that image is Rose Cottage and in the top corner, that's surely Bluebell Wood, looking much larger than it is today." In the left hand corner they could just make out a small drawing of an ancient tower, similar to the ruined castle tower near the lake. There were no farm buildings shown on the map, but it showed two paths , one leading to the south side of the wood, the other from the tower, skirting the water meadows and following the stream back to the bridge.

It was an old map of his very own farm, drawn maybe two hundred years ago or more. He found the next sheet and laid it out beside the first one. They

saw that the two fitted together, because there was the path passing through the wood and coming out the other side. The line of the path ended in what looked like a rough, childish drawing of a quarry. Their gaze was drawn to the middle of the quarry, where someone had marked a large 'X'.

"I know where that quarry is!" he shouted, nearly choking on his hot coffee. "It's very overgrown now and hasn't been used for hundreds of years or more. Certainly not in my lifetime or that of my dad, or even his dad before him, as far as I know.

"Trees have grown up all around where the quarry used to be, but if I remember correctly from when I was a boy, I came upon a clearing in the wood where a huge oak tree must have once stood. In those days there was just a huge stump remaining from the original tree. Looking at this drawing I guess that stump coincides with this X mark here," he said, pointing to the centre of Bluebell Wood.

The two youngsters turned and looked at each other, said nothing but smiled, not wanting to give any secrets away.

"I only went there once, Lucy, and it was on that visit that I saw what was left of this huge tree stump and those bits of rusty old machinery. It's pretty scary down there and I have often thought to myself that there are 'things' living in that wood. I don't need to go there now, so I keep well away from it. You shouldn't go there either," he told them.

A sudden look of despair came over their faces. All the excitement and now this, surely he wouldn't stop them from visiting Bluebell Wood? That would be a disaster for them. As they sat listening to their dear friend talking about the plans in front of him and his life as a young boy, they remembered all that had happened since finding the cave and the beautiful mermaid at Lyme Regis. Was all this going to end in failure because Mr Grundy didn't like them going to the clearing and because he thought there were 'strange goings on' in the wood?

That night everyone went to bed early, not because they were especially tired, but because they were all feeling a little down in spirits, especially Lucy and William. For the last two days they had been so excited about the possibility of finding treasure. But not this time, they thought, just a ring and some faded old maps.

"Don't forget the sword and the uniform Sis," said William, trying hard to encourage his sister, but more in hope than expectation.

As Lucy lay on top of her bed, writing up her diary, she asked William"Why have you been so quiet all afternoon and evening? You've hardly said a word to anyone. It upsets me when you're like this." When William was quiet she had no one to talk to, and Mrs Grundy wouldn't really understand because she's a grown up, and grown ups don't understand young people, do they?

"Lucy," he eventually replied, "I've been thinking all afternoon and evening and an idea has come to me." He turned over in his top bunk and peered over the edge to look down at her. "I've been thinking so hard, because there is something that worries me about this whole story. Would you like me to tell you what I think?"

"Oh yes please, go on," said Lucy now more enthusiastic and propping herself up on one elbow. She was really awake now. If William had an idea then she wanted to know about it. Sharing their thoughts about most things was something they were good at.

During the next twenty minutes or so, as William recalled, step by step, all that had happened during the day, Lucy became more and more fascinated. Maybe it was because William told the day's events in such an interesting way. In fact she was so interested that she got out of her bed and climbed up into William's bed so that she could hear more clearly what he was saying.

"Tell me again," William, she pleaded, "because I was only half awake when you started telling me the first time."

So he repeated all that was scrambling around in his head, about the maps, about Bluebell Wood and the clearing. And of course, about the strange noises Mr Grundy spoke about. He told her what he thought about the plans, but he had no idea what the key in the mahogany box was for, or what the ring with the dragon image meant. That was a mystery, he told her. They would need to solve it and who better to solve it than William, with Lucy's help of course.

Over the next half hour William described to Lucy the ideas that were still flying around in his head; flying, but getting nowhere. She listened with rapt curiosity, not stopping him once to ask a question, which was unusual for Lucy. She was known at school for interrupting but it was because she wanted to know more, not because she was naughty or rude.

"Was there a possibility," he said, thinking aloud, "that the mystery machine, what ever it is, was built in the ancient quarry shown on the map, a long time ago by someone who went to sea? Or, might the person have been a sailor at the time that he built the machine? He picked the quarry near his home so that no one would discover his secret while he was building it.

"Then something important happened, or maybe there was a disaster. He might have had to go away, leaving the machine in the quarry. But as no one knew about it he had to hide the drawings and the key thing in his mahogany box." He paused to let his ideas sink in. "And maybe, the ring will give us a clue to his name, or who he was."

"That seems a very far fetched story, William, but I like it," said Lucy. "But how did they get into the sea chest?"

"Well, he could have gone to sea in a warship, you know, just like the ones in Papo's picture hanging over the fireplace in their lounge. Papo told me that in the olden days, about two hundred or more years ago, important sailors put all their possessions into wooden sea chests that they took to sea with them," said William, warming to his story. "I've also seen pictures of them in my adventure books."

"Yes, but what do you think happened then?" asked Lucy, with a frown as she followed the story.

"Well, I think there must have been a huge storm one night, the ship floundered on the rocks near Lyme Regis and it sank and everyone drowned." However, before the ship sank, the sailor who owned the chest quickly wrote the message, put it in the bottle and threw it into the sea, hoping someone would find it."

"I can understand that, but what about the sea chest?" asked Lucy impatiently. "How did it get into the cottage attic?"

William was now well into his story and the more he thought about it, the more it all made sense to him. But would the others believe him?

"Well Lucy, as the ship broke up on the rocks I think the wooden chest

After the shipwreck

would have floated ashore on the tide along with the bottle." he explained. "Wood floats, you know." Lucy nodded.

"Somehow, both were washed into the cave, where the chest could have been found by smugglers and then carried to Rose Cottage. In those days, Lucy, there was no farm here, just the old cottage by the stone bridge that we saw drawn on that ancient map."

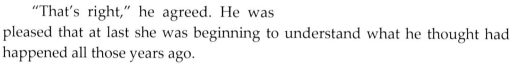

"I bet whoever smuggled it out of the cave failed to find the bottle." Lucy butted in eagerly.

"That's right," he agreed. He was pleased that at last she was beginning to understand what he thought had happened all those years ago.

Lucy sat upright on the bed, excited by their discoveries, and then continued to tell the story the way she thought it might have happened. "Then William, whoever found the chest in the cave, carried it to the cottage but they couldn't open it, so they hid it in the attic for safety. Do you know, William, in the olden days if you were caught smuggling, it was a hanging offence?"

William shuddered at the thought of it. Who wanted to be strung up on a tree branch to rot, just for stealing a sea chest or some bottles of rum? He knew that happened two hundred years ago, but not now, thank goodness.

As she sat on the bed beside him, thinking about the story, William's ideas seemed very plausible. In fact, she could not have thought of a better story if she had tried to herself and she certainly had been trying that evening before they went to bed.

"I think we'll have to tell Mr Grundy about our ideas," said Lucy and William agreed that they would tell the adults the next day.

They got up early next morning and full of excitement, walked across the yard and into the kitchen for breakfast. William saw the first group of early morning rooks flying off over the Dutch barn to find their breakfast, a reminder to them of the day to come. It was going to be a warmish day, he thought, without too much cloud to spoil things for them.

"You're up with the lark you two. Couldn't you sleep last night?" asked Mrs Grundy, as she broke two fresh eggs into the frying pan for Mr Grundy's breakfast. The sizzling sound of the eggs in the bacon fat made their mouths water. They suddenly realized that all yesterday's excitement had made them very hungry. They wondered if Mrs Grundy would give them some bacon too.

They pulled their chairs up to the table and looked at Mrs Grundy, who was smiling at them as she moved the bacon around the pan amongst the frying eggs. She waited for one of them to say something, knowing by the look on their faces that they wanted to share their thoughts with her.

"Well then, I know you want to tell me something. What is it then?" She flipped bacon fat over the sizzling eggs. "I know you two are up to something, so what is it?" Just then, the kitchen door from the hallway creaked open and a rather tired-looking Mr Grundy came into the kitchen. He had an early morning look on his face.

"Morning! You two are up early, couldn't you sleep?" He rubbed the sleep out of his eyes as he took his seat at the table. It was pretty obvious to that he had had little sleep during the night, but the bacon and eggs were ready and the children knew that with his cooked breakfast, Mr Grundy would start the day in a good frame of mind, a bit like Papo.

"Do you know," he said, turning to the two children, "I've been lying awake all night thinking about this mystery. I just have no answer to the puzzle of the sea chest, or the mahogany box, and certainly not that key gadget and the ring. Also, what are the maps trying to tell us? It's a complete puzzle to me and I bet it's the same for you two, eh?"

Lucy nudged her brother. "Go on, tell them William," she said excitedly through a full mouth of cereal.

"Tell us what?" quizzed Mr Grundy, as he sat down to eat his breakfast. All this chit chat was going nowhere.

Mrs Grundy had also cooked them their breakfast and was waiting to place the large white plates in front of them once the cereals had been eaten.

William plucked up the courage to speak and while the others sat eating their breakfast, he recounted his ideas about the sea chest. He told them what he thought the maps were telling them and he explained his theory about the ship wreck and what could have happened to the chest.

"Bless my soul! I don't believe it," said Mr Grundy, with a look of amazement on his face as he popped the last piece of egg into his mouth and wiped his moustache with a hanky.

"Here am I, awake all night, unable to sleep, trying to work out how all these things fit together, and you come with these great ideas William. Well done lad.

"We don't have any proof but I think your ideas are a good way for us to start to work this out. We have the maps and that ring and there are the old drawings of a machine contraption, or something or other! Then there's that clearing in Bluebell Wood. Now that really baffles me, so it does."

"Now let me get this right," he went on, "are you also telling me that the clearing in the centre of Bluebell Wood used to be the old quarry all those years ago? But now it's all filled in and overgrown?"

"Yes I am," said a confident William, looking very pleased with himself as he ate another piece of thick buttered toast, this time with tomato sauce all over it. He just loved tomato sauce.

"Not only that Mr Grundy," said William, "but I believe I might know where our mystery machine is. The trouble is, I don't know what it is or what it was used for." At this stage William had decided to keep its real identity to himself. Mustn't give too much away at the beginning, always keep something back just in case, and to keep people interested.

"Bless my soul again!" exclaimed Mr Grundy, this time wiping his mouth on the back of his sleeve. "Can I have another cup of tea please dear?"

"You're full of ideas this morning, aren't you William?" But William was still not sure whether the old man believed him, even though his ideas seemed very plausible. The question was, he thought to himself as he gulped down a mouthful of hot chocolate, where is the machine now, if it still exists after all these years?

William had already decided to keep those ideas to himself. He didn't want to tell them everything, not even Lucy. Instead, he said it would be a few days before he thought he might have the answer for them. Hopefully, if all goes well, there might be an answer before their holiday ended and they had to return to Beech House, their parents and school.

Mr Grundy's mood had perked up a little, especially after his cooked breakfast, which he ate with great relish and gusto as usual. A fry-up was his favourite meal and always put him in a good mood for the rest of the day, a bit like Papo the children thought. "I'll have two cups of coffee," he said

"Well, bless my soul again!"

140

to his wife, "with toast and marmalade. No, make that one marmalade and one honey, please."

The children hurriedly finished off the rest of their breakfast, excused themselves and went to put on their coats and boots. They had things to do. Secret things, that were not for grown-ups to wonder about or get involved in.

Before they could meet Mr Fudge that evening they had other important jobs to do. One of them, and they hadn't yet decided who, would have to walk to the village, four miles away, to post their letter home, telling Mummy and Daddy all that was happening. It also sent their love, of course, and said how much they were looking forward to coming home.

"William," said Lucy, "we'll have to tell Mr Fudge the story from beginning to end, you know that don't you? That's going to take time, but it's essential to get his advice and his reaction to our ideas before we do anything else, don't you agree?"

He nodded. Would Mr Fudge believe them, he wondered, and did he know anything about the sailor? They thought that was unlikely because Mr Fudge was only made a few years ago. But he was extraordinarily special and knew the Little People well, so somehow he might also know about the sailor; a sort of sixth sense, thought William.

They also needed to chat to Benjamin after talking to Fudge. They would have to confide in him and tell him all about William's ideas, especially about the clearing. Benjamin would then tell Little People and they might help to solve the mystery.

As they talked to each other it was obvious that the biggest problem would be letting Mr Grundy know about the Little People. There were two questions that had to be answered: would they agree to meet him, and would he meet them? The Little People were wary of humans at the best of time.

Later that evening after a day pottering around the farm, and after an early supper of beans on toast, they walked over Lower Meadow in the fading light to meet Mr Fudge in the potato field. He was so pleased to see them and even more pleased when William told him about what they'd found in the attic. William then explained his ideas to his friend.

The wise old scarecrow listened intently, looking his young friend full in the eye as William retold his theory. There were no interruptions as William carefully explained everything, being particularly careful not to leave anything out. When he had finished, the scarecrow turned to Lucy.

"I want a meeting soon. I suggest tomorrow at midnight. We need to discuss William's ideas with everyone who could or might be involved. We must do this before you go back home," he insisted, "it's important, in fact it's an emergency." He waved his arms excitedly, as they'd never seen before.

Lucy thought it would be a big meeting if all his friends were invited, but she said nothing, knowing that Mr Fudge was very wise. If he wanted all his country friends to know, then they must know.

"Tomorrow at midnight we'll all gather in Bluebell Wood," said Mr Fudge earnestly. "I think we should meet at the clearing. Benjamin can carry me there, which I don't care for very much, but it must be done. All the Little People can listen to William and then have their say about his ideas. What do you think to that, you two?"

How could they possibly disagree? Lucy thought Mr Fudge sounded very stern, but then she realised how important this meeting was going to be for everyone, not just

"The wise old scarecrow listened intently as William explained ..."

them. They said good night to their friend and made their way back across Lower Meadow, not saying a word to each other until they arrived back at the farm yard. Lucy then turned and faced her brother.

"William, do you think they will help us?" she asked.

He thought a bit, then looked her in the eyes he said with a slight hesitation in his voice, "Whatever we do Lucy, we must never break our friendship with the Little People or any of Mr Fudge's country friends. If we did, if we lost their friendship, then staying at Rose Cottage wouldn't be the same, ever again, would it?"

She gave him a cuddle and knew he was right. But was it worth the risk?

"You know Sis, I'm a bit scared about tis meeting, but I don't want to let any of them down. You're right, they would never speak to us again and that would be the end of our holidays here at the farm, for ever. Before tomorrow night I will have to think about what I am going to say and how I'm going to say it. I've never had to do this before. Would you help me please?" He looked at his sister for reassurance.

The thought of that happening, of maybe loosing all her new friends and no more happy times at the cottage was more than Lucy could bear. They took off their shoes and crept quietly into the kitchen to find both the Grundys fast asleep in their chairs with their feet up in front of the Aga. Without waking them and as quiet as mice, they each took two of their favourite biscuits from the biscuit tin on the cupboard. Pouring themselves a glass of cold fresh milk from the jug, they crept out again, as quietly as field mice in a house full of hens. Crossing the yard on tiptoe they entered their 'home from home', as Lucy liked to call it.

A quick wash, teeth brushed, clothes put in neat piles at the bottom of the bunk bed, then the two young children climbed into their warm comfy beds.

"I know we have all day tomorrow to think about what you're going to say, but we should think about it now, just for a few minutes before we go to sleep," said Lucy. But there was no sound from the top bunk except a steady breathing. He's asleep, she thought, and with that she turned over, snuggled under the duvet and was soon fast asleep herself.

That night she dreamed pleasant dreams of summer holidays and farm teas, walking across the meadows full of buttercups and daisies and playing with the Little People in their cavern. At one point a pony entered her dream but soon vanished.

It was different outside. The fields around the farm were certainly not asleep. There was always a lot of night activity in the countryside, which most humans never see or hear, but it goes on all the same. The neighbour's cows were quietly chewing the cud after a long day grazing.

The sly old vixen fox from Bluebell Wood would be teaching her two cubs how to catch their own food. They would try something easy to start with and where better than the hen house behind the Dutch barn? There would be a plentiful supply of fat hens, if only she and her cubs could get at them. But they were out of luck, yet again. All the hens and the noisy cockerel that bossed them about were safely locked up for the night. Maybe a visit to the stream near the bridge might turn up a fat frog or two for the cubs. It wasn't that they liked frogs but they were hungry, and chasing hopping frogs was a good way to teach her cubs to hunt.

You never know, she thought the old vixen as she led her cubs through the yard towards the stream, there just might be a few fat mice looking for their own supper in the long grass by the bank, Or, if they were really lucky, a plump, sleeping pheasant. Now, that would be a treat for two young hungry cubs. There were many possibilities and there were at least another five hours before the sun would wake the countryside and she would have to lead her youngsters back to their den.

Somehow the word was reaching all those who had to know: there was to be an important meeting in Bluebell Wood tomorrow night at midnight, sharp. Everyone must be there, especially the Little People.

Chapter 11

The Mystery Unfolds in Bluebell Wood

Next morning after breakfast and before Mr Grundy started his day's work, William told him as much as he thought he should know. Not everything though, especially not about the Little People. That particular part of the story would have to wait until after the meeting tonight in the cavern. Once the meeting was over he could complete the story for him, which he desperately wanted to do as he never liked keeping secrets from his friend.

During the day as he helped Mr Grundy with odd jobs around the farm, he thought about what he should say to the Little People and how he could persuade them that he should be allowed to try out his ideas. He knew that everything would depend on how well he spoke. Then would they agree to let Mr Grundy into their secret too. Both were very difficult problems to overcome.

He came in early for lunch so that he could sit and think about this evening. Lucy had a great idea for him that he knew would help him to perform this worrying task.

"Why don't you write the main points down, William, in the order that you should tell them? You can then hold the notes in your hand as you speak. This will make sure you leave nothing out by mistake and it will also give the impression that you have given a lot of thought and attention to detail, wanting to be accurate."

Wrinkling his brow, he thought that was brilliant. "That's a great idea Lucy." And he went off to look for a piece of paper and pencil. By that evening he was pretty sure he knew exactly what he would say, and how he would say it in front of everybody.

It was a very complicated story and there was a lot to sort out, but when he handed the list to Lucy, he was pretty certain that he had decided which were the most important things.

The list had just six main headings that he and Lucy had decided he should concentrate on:

1. *Finding the glass bottle in the cave.*
2. *Working out the meaning of the scroll.*
3. *Meeting the Grundys and Mr Fudge.*
4. *Finding the sea chest and mahogany box.*
5. *Working out the mystery of the plans.*
6. *How the Little People could help them.*

Lucy thought to herself as she read the list for the third time that if William is going to mention all these things in detail, then it will be a very long meeting indeed. Far too long for the Little People to concentrate, and too long for dear old Mr Fudge. Somehow, William will have to make it shorter but still tell them the main parts of the story.

She mentioned this to him and the two of them agreed what to leave out, what to leave in and the final order of things. He would still cover the six points but in a shorter time. He was so pleased with the final result that he gave her a hug to show his appreciation.

That evening Mrs Grundy surprised everyone, which she loved to do. For supper, she had cooked one of her special beef pies covered with thick golden brown flaky pastry. Dished up with the pie was a bowl of mixed green vegetables and smooth mashed potatoes grown on the farm, with a huge dollop of creamy butter melting slowly all over it. They sat at the table, their mouths watering and tummies rumbled in anticipation as they watched her serve each plate of pie. Before they were able to pile on the vegetables, she poured hot rich brown gravy all over the meat. This was the children's absolute favourite!

For a special treat to finish off their supper, she gave each of them a plate of mixed fruit jelly covered with sweet hot custard, liberally laced with sugar.

When supper was over they were full to bursting point. Mr Grundy staggered up from the table to sit in his favourite chair. William just sat at the table day-dreaming, with his hands across his stomach. It'll soon be midnight, he thought to himself, and then the fun will really begin for him and Lucy.

That evening when the clock struck nine and it was time for bed, they both decided they would only pretend to go to bed. Instead, they would keep their clothes on, except for their shoes of course. When the time came they could quickly get out of bed, put their shoes on and make for Bluebell Wood without anyone noticing. That was the plan, but would it work? That was the question. They said good night to the elderly couple, thanking them for the fantastic supper. It was quiet in the yard as they made for their 'home' with great excitement and a little trepidation, particularly for William who would be bearing the brunt of the meeting.

They kept a light on in their room as they lay on top of their duvets, both thinking about the forthcoming gathering at the clearing and trying hard to imagine what it was going to be like. They'd both been many times to the cavern, but never for an occasion like this one.

A few hours later Lucy looked at her watch as the two of them crossed Lower Meadow, making towards the wood by the light of a watery moon. They hoped to see or hear the barn owl and her mate but all was quiet and not even the rooks stirred. Nothing was stirring tonight, not even a mouse in the undergrowth. It was half past eleven.

They were in good time and had no need to rush as they arrived at the badger's hole in the hedge. This was their usual way of getting into Bluebell Wood. They scrambled through the gap without catching their clothes on any bramble thorns. They quickened their pace as they walked down the twisting path in the dark with the torch beam lighting the narrow path. They had no fear of the wood because they had come this way so many times before. Arriving at the edge of the clearing, they stopped, staring in amazement at the sight that confronted them.

Under the canopy of thick overhanging branches the clearing was ablaze with yellow twinkling lights. The oak tree stump shone like a fairy cathedral at night, its broken trunk pointing to the heavens. Sitting quietly in a circle around the base of the stump, waiting patiently, were all the Little People, large ones and small ones, young and old. They were all there, along with their country friends from the fields and woods. Lucy realised now why it had been so quiet when they crossed Lower Meadow, they were all here. Even the two barn owls from the Dutch barn sat on one of the lower branches, so still they could have been stuffed birds in a Victorian glass case.

She realised that the light in the clearing didn't come from the moon, but from thousands and thousands of fireflies that the Little People had brought up from the cavern below. They had hung them around the trees and over the stump to light up the clearing so that everyone could see everyone else. This was magical, she thought to herself as the two of them walked slowly towards the gathered masses. Well, it felt like masses.

"Here they are everyone," shouted out Benjamin, jumping up from the ground where he had been sitting and talking to Mr Fudge. He was conveniently propped up against a tree like a king on his throne so that everybody could see him from where they sat. "We're all here, and looking

forward to what you want to tell us William." Benjamin clapped his hands for silence.

For the first time that day, in fact, for the first time in his life, William felt sick in the pit of his stomach. This must be what real fear is like, he thought

"You'll be alright big brother," said Lucy, and she squeezed his hand to reassure him. They moved forward through the circle of Little People, who made way for them. William remembered the first time he had to face a fast bowler when playing cricket for the school. He had that same feeling in his tummy then as he had now, but he had dealt with it that time and he could deal with it this time too.

They stood next to Mr Fudge. He coughed, not one of his best coughs, but good enough to stop all the chatting and squeaking around him. Not long now, he thought. William waited for his turn to speak, shaking slightly but not badly enough for anyone to notice. Thank goodness Lucy had helped him to write the headings down on the piece of paper.

"Tonight is a very special night for all of us." Mr Fudge had started to speak and everyone had turned to look at him, even the animals and birds.

"William and Lucy, our two young human friends, who you all know well, have something very special to say. But, before they do, I want to tell you that their friendship with all of us in the wood and the fields is the most important thing for them, and it must not be harmed by whatever happens this evening."

"It was quite dark in the clearing ..."

His words silenced the clearing, even the grass and the trees. Mr Fudge then continued, "I would like William now to tell us all about his ideas, please. Would you come and stand next to me, so we can all see and hear you clearly?" Under his breath he whispered in William's ear not to talk too fast as some of the younger Little People might find it hard to follow what he was saying. William smiled and nodded towards him in agreement.

William got up off the grass, eased his tight jeans down his legs for more comfort, held his head up and pulled his shoulders back. He walked towards the stump like an army general about to give the talk of his life to his troops. Taking the small piece of paper out of his pocket as he went, he decided to stand on the lower step that leads down into the cavern. From there he could look across all their heads to Lucy, who was now standing at the back of the gathering.

She gave him a small wave and a big smile which made him feel good. He looked at the paper, slightly shaking in his hand, took a deep breath, counted up to five and started to talk.

"Hello everyone," and then he told them about their first meeting and all the times that he and Lucy had spent with them playing, dancing and telling them stories about the way humans live. He told them about the cave at Lyme Regis, of seeing the mermaid and finding the glass bottle. Of course, he mentioned Mamo and Papo, and Mummy and Daddy, and their home at Beech House, but more important he told them all about the poem and how Lucy had found the farm on the map, the excitement of finding the sea chest in the attic at Rose Cottage and last of all, about what it contained.

As soon as he got to the part about the machine, a murmur rose amongst the Little People, which got louder and louder. Oh dear, what had he said to worry them? Benjamin called for hush and the noise quietened down.

By now he was quite relaxed and was really enjoying his story telling. As he continued to talk about the machine the chattering noise rose again.

"Quiet please, quiet please," implored Mr Fudge, trying to stop the noise that was drowing out what William was saying. "Please let William continue with his story." The loud hubbub subsided and everyone listened to what he was going to say next.

William now came to the most important part of his story. This was the bit that worried him most because he had no idea how the Little People would react to his ideas. What would their Leader say?

Looking around the circle of friends for their reactions, he told them again about the possibility of a machine and about the odd bits of metal he had seen lying around when visiting the cavern. He explained about the land maps and the drawings of the machine and why he thought that the machine was buried somewhere in their cavern. He told them that he thought the bits of metal were part of this buried machine and that somewhere, if they looked hard enough, they might find it.

No one said a word when he finished. There was complete silence in the clearing. Everyone was mesmerised by what he had said to them, except for the leader of the Little People. He had been listening to William, nodding every few minutes as if he, and only he, knew something that the others didn't know.

After what seemed like ages, the Leader moved towards him. William felt very lonely and apprehensive. In a quiet voice that everyone could hear the Leader said, "William, you are a very clever young human," and he touched him on his arm for reassurance. William relaxed as the Leader started to talk slowly but very carefully, because he wanted everyone

A machine buried somewhere in the cavern ...

to understand what he was about to tell them.

"We are all grateful to Mr Fudge because he introduced William and Lucy to us. Through knowing them and becoming their friends, I believe young William and his sister Lucy have solved the mystery that we Little People have been grappling with for the last two hundred years."

"Don't forget Mr Grundy the farmer," piped up a voice at the back of the circle. Everyone laughed and William and Lucy felt relieved that things were going well so far.

The leader continued, "What William has told us tonight is very nearly correct, but not completely so. I would like to tell you about parts of the story that William has no knowledge of.

"Yes, it is true, there was once an important sailor who lived at Rose Cottage. The legend tells us that he built it with stone from the quarry behind Bluebell Wood. The story has come down to us over the last two hundred years and recalls that our ancestors were somehow involved with his ancestors. That's all we know. We do not know why we helped him or how he helped us. We believe that when he found out that we lived in the dark, he designed what he called 'a machine' to give us light. This machine, which William has been talking to us about, still exists. We, the few elders of the Little People tribe also think it is a 'light making machine', but it could be for something completely different. We don't know.

"In its day, a 'light making machine' would have been a fantastic invention. No one had ever produced artificial light before. Underneath this clearing where we are now sitting, buried deep in a hidden part of the cavern that none of you have seen, is what is left of that machine. Only a few of us Little People have known about it. Unfortunately we can't make it work and our ancestors told us that it never has worked. We are not clever enough to make it work without human help. I think the time has now arrived, because I believe William will be able to help us make it work, whether it's a 'light making machine' or something completely different.

"William understands human writing and the drawings. He is very practical at constructing models and I know he will show us what needs to be done, won't you William?"

"What happened to the sailor?" asked Mr Fudge when the Leader had stopped speaking.

"Our verbal history tells us that 'our sailor friend' had to go to sea and was never seen again", replied the Leader. "That's why the machine was never finished. We hid it in a part of the cavern that is never visited by our tribe. We

"Legend tells us of a machine to give us light"

older ones hoped that one day someone could help us to make it work. I think this day has now arrived, don't you Mr Fudge?"

The Little People erupted with joy and their friends joined in with the excitement. Had they won over the hearts and minds of these wonderful creatures? William looked at Lucy, Lucy looked at Mr Fudge and he in turn looked at Benjamin. This was their dream come true. This was going to be their way of helping the Little People for the way they looked after the countryside and had befriended them and others in the past. Lucy remembered what her Mamo had said to her sometime ago, 'Lucy, never forget, one good turn always deserves another good turn.' Mamo was right, as usual.

With that very long speech now over, William was able to sit down at the bottom of the steps and relax. The Little People clapped and stamped their feet with happiness. They didn't hear Benjamin shout out that he thought there should now be a feast to celebrate all this good news.

Before William could get up and move away from the throng of bodies pressed around him, Lucy ran up to her brother and wrapped her arms around his neck to give him the biggest kiss and a huge long hug.

"Well done little brother!" she said with such pride that William was quite surprised. He knew deep down that Lucy loved him very much, even though he didn't like her calling him 'little brother'. He would naturally prefer 'big brother', but this time he would ignore it and not make a fuss. Right now he was too happy and just kept thinking to himself, what would have happened if the leader of the Little People had not been so pleased with his ideas. This 'light making machine' must be very important to them and he hoped that he could help to make it work.

A thought suddenly flashed through his head, what if the machine is not for making light, but was intended to do something else? The Leader had said he wasn't sure, because they had no written words to tell them about their past history. There was only the drawing on parchment they had found in the chest. He paused, then murmured to himself, no, it must be for light making. And with that he got up, stretched his legs and looked around for Mr Fudge to ask him how he thought it all went.

"I don't think I could have done better myself, William," said Mr Fudge. There was no 'well done', or, 'that was excellent', not even a 'thank you', he just passed the whole event off as if it was an everyday occurrence. William knew he'd done a good job and had managed to put all the important information across to everyone and it would have been nice to have received a little praise from Mr Fudge. But then he was only a scarecrow!

The night had passed and although it was getting towards morning, Lucy and William were not going to leave the party before they had enjoyed themselves. A great array of goodies had been brought up from the cavern by the younger Little People. The magnificent display of food reminded them again of the happy party enjoyed by everyone in the potato field.

There was something to eat for everyone, except the two barn owls. They flew off looking for their own food, which the Little People were not able to give them. Laughing, Benjamin said that the owls were on special diets and couldn't eat fruit and nuts.

Lucy saw William talking quietly to Mr Fudge and approached them, humming to herself.

"Where do we go from here you two?" she asked. She had noticed that Mr Fudge had said very little all night, but the look on his turnip face showed that he was very happy with the way

things were turning out. The Little People were happy, he was happy, and it was obvious to all that William was happy too.

He reacted to her question with an air of authority which amused Lucy and somewhat surprised William. "We will need another meeting in the cavern soon, so the Leader can show you this buried machine thing. Unfortunately, due to my condition, I can't be there as I have duties to perform in the potato field but Benjamin will be free and he can report back to me all the decisions you've made about what to do next."

Before anyone could respond to what had just been said, he continued, "I hope you can do this before the end of your holiday William. It's essential that it's done quickly, in fact quicker than that."

"So do I," answered William, now feeling more relaxed after eating all that food. He still felt a bit sore that Fudge had not shown much enthusiasm for his talk, but what the heck, Lucy was happy, the Leader was obviously happy, so why worry about poor old Fudge?

"Can we tell the Grundys what's happened tonight?" they both asked him at once.

"If Benjamin thinks it will be safe to tell them, then we'll do just that, but only after we have asked the Little People first. I don't think it will be a problem, do you Benjamin?" he enquired of his friend.

Benjamin nodded his head in agreement but said nothing. They would all meet in the cavern tomorrow afternoon after lunch. It was a good time of the day because the Grundys would be having their after lunch snooze and it would be easy to have an hour away from the farm without upsetting them, or having to tell them where they were going.

"Remember everybody, we go back to school in a few days time," Lucy said, reminding them all again about the urgency of the next gathering.

Two happy youngsters wished everyone good night and made their way out of the wood, ducking through the badger's hole, across Top Meadow and back to their cold beds. They didn't mind as they took off their shoes and climbed under the cold duvets. It had been a super night. William had surpassed himself and his big sister was so proud of him. Two very tired but happy people fell into a deep sleep.

"Three more days and then it's back to school Sis," said William to his sister the next day as he wandered aimlessly around the farm yard, wondering what to do during the morning to waste time before they met all their friends back in the cavern that afternoon.

"I know what you can do, why don't you go fishing down by the bridge. You like doing that William," she said, acting quite grown up. "You might even find that grey heron down there. He always seems to know where the best fish can be found this time of year."

"He'll just fly off when I get there," mumbled William, hands in pockets as he kicked a large lump of earth that had fallen off one of the tractor tyres. It flew across the yard, shattering into small pieces and flying off in all directions. "I know, I think I'll go and see if Mrs Grundy wants some help in the kitchen. If she's cooking there'll be left overs and I'm jolly hungry because I didn't eat all my breakfast this morning. I was so excited after last night." He wandered across to the cottage and through the open back door.

Lucy decided that as she had all morning and nothing planned, she would start to pack their cases. On this occasion she would also pack William's, as he tended just to throw everything into his case, just like all untidy boys. Packing the cases took up most of the morning. She took her time sorting things out the way she wanted them and she was pleased with the final results. She really hated packing at the end of each holiday. She and William always found it difficult to settle back into school routine and family life after all the freedom they were given on the farm. But there was always the next holiday to look forward to and lots of things to do in between.

Surprisingly she managed to squeeze all their clothes into two cases and a large black holdall that was filled with shoes, some bigger items and some dirty washing that she couldn't ask Mrs Grundy to do, so near to the end of the holiday.

Mrs Grundy had agreed to give them an early lunch. Not that she knew what they were up to, but she knew something was happening because for once William was very quiet, hardly speaking a word all morning. Maybe he's unhappy about going home. He's a strange boy at times, she thought to herself. Normally he's such a chatter box at lunchtime, telling us what he would be doing in the afternoon, but not today. Something was afoot, she thought and wondered what it could be.

Every day after lunch , Mrs Grundy would wash up the dishes, William would dry them and Lucy would put them away in one of the glass-fronted cupboards. Today was no different and soon the kitchen was spick and span, everything put away and time for her afternoon snooze.

Chapter 12

The Lost Machine

They had found their way to the clearing so many times over the last two years that it took them no time at all today to repeat the journey. They both could have walked down the path to the tree stump blindfolded, if asked. The door was there and open as she expected. Bending down slightly, Lucy pushed it further open with her left hand and they both ducked their heads as they climbed down the steps and into the brightly lit cavern.

Looking around it seemed as if all their friends were there waiting for them to arrive. One of the endearing qualities that Benjamin had noticed about Lucy and William over the months that he had known them was they were never late. That was something the Little People appreciated even though they didn't posses watches or clocks or any way of telling the time. Somehow, they just knew what time of day or night it was. They thought it was a bit sad that Mr Fudge couldn't be with them, but they knew Benjamin would tell him all about this very important meeting.

As they moved further into the cavern they saw Benjamin standing in the middle of the crowd of Little People. Of course, it was his turn to be in charge today, not one of the Leaders. Very quickly he had all the Little People settled on the floor, except the Leader, who was nowhere to be seen. Then, quite unexpectedly, he appeared and stood next to Benjamin and waved to William to come and join him.

Lucy slowly edged her way behind the crowd of Little People until she was opposite William and could look at him to give him encouragement if he needed it. After yesterday's talk he now had plenty of confidence. Once you've done it, he thought to himself, you could cope with anything that comes your way. She sat down. The Leader of the Little People lifted his short hairy arms, waving them about to ask for quiet.

Although he did feel quite confident, William still got goose bumps all down his arms and his throat was getting very dry with excitement. He looked over to his big sister for reassurance. She gave him a huge smile and he began to feel less worried about the prospect of looking for the buried machine. What a thrill it was going to be, not only for him, but all the others. What are they going to find?

He wondered how the rest of the tribe would react because it was as new to them as to him. As he waited patiently, he thought about all the things that they had discovered recently. There was the sea chest, the drawings, the sword and uniform, that key object, and many others.

Benjamin spoke up so everyone could hear him. In his best voice he said, "I would like all of you to stay here except William and Lucy. Your Leader will take us deep into the cavern where no one has been before and will be showing us where the light making machine is buried. William will inspect it and then tell us what needs to be done to make it work."

There was a lot of murmuring and nodding in agreement, but it was obvious that some were not happy about it. Lucy felt sorry for them; some would have liked to have gone with them deeper into the cavern, where no one in the present tribe had been before. It wasn't often they had excitement in their lives like this and they didn't want to miss it. But Benjamin had spoken and they must also obey their Leader, who had delegated this important exploration to Benjamin. Tribal law demanded that whatever their feelings, they must obey at all times.

Within a few minutes the discord and murmuring had settled down. The four of them left the Little People chattering excitedly amongst themselves in the main cavern. William checked that he had the plans in his pocket and the torch, which would be needed in the confines of the narrow underground passageways. He followed Benjamin and the Leader down a dark corridor away from the brightly lit main cavern. This dark world was all new to him; he thought a rabbit warren might be like it, but much bigger. There were tunnels going off in all directions but no sign posts to show where you are, or how far you have gone.

The surface of the floor under his shoes felt like hard compact earth and the walls and ceiling felt smooth to his touch where they had been worn by years of constant stone rubbing. As she followed the two in front, bending her neck to miss the ceiling, Lucy wondered to herself who had created such a place? The Little People weren't allowed in this part of their underground home, so who in the distant past created it and when and why?

She walked close to William, almost touching him in the semi-darkness, because she didn't want to get lost in the labyrinth of corridors and passageways. They only had one torch, which Benjamin was using at the front. "Why didn't they bring more with them?" she mumbled to herself.

She realised that it was easy for the leader because he could see in the dark. It was a skill which William and Lucy had not been able to learn, even though the Little People had tried so very hard to teach them. It had been one of the skills they had promised to show them when they had first met. But it wasn't to be, as it was beyond the ability of humans to learn.

They walked on, stumbling down twisting corridors and getting the impression that they were getting deeper and deeper underground. It was strange, but the air was fresh and there was no smell of decaying vegetation, which she had expected so deep under the forest floor. They turned left, then right and then left again so many times that she lost count. Eventually, the floor of the stopped sloping downwards and opened out into what seemed like a wide room.

"Have we arrived? Where is the machine?" she asked the Leader, who remained silent, not answering her questions.

At the far end of what Lucy had thought of as a room, she saw that the wall was covered in what looked like a curtain suspended from the roof to the floor. It seemed to be made of faded and intertwined grass, woven with dusty brownish reeds, all draped over a pole. It covered the wall completely and was obviously hiding something jolly big behind it. The curtain looked so frail and delicate, and made Lucy shudder because as she stared at it she could see it was covered in massive cobwebs, the biggest and most ugly she had ever seen in her life. By the light of Benjamin's torch she saw hundreds of creepy crawlies of all sizes and shapes scampering away from the light, looking for dark crannies to escape into.

She shuddered. Her mouth went dry and there was an awful temptation to scream, but she managed to hold her breath until the beam from Benjamin's torch frightened all the ugly creatures away into the corners and cracks in the surrounding earth walls.

"This is where our machine is, William, over there behind this old curtain," said the Leader, approaching the curtain slowly. "It's been hidden from view for over two hundred and fifty years, waiting for someone like you to show us how to make it work."

"William?" there was silence. No one spoke in the eerie quietness that wrapped itself around them in this deep underground place.

"Yes, I'm here," he said, his voice croaking and his body shaking a little, in fact, quite a lot if the truth be known. Doubts suddenly appeared in his mind. He wondered what he was doing here and if he could really help them. He was scared but didn't want to show it. For the first time he wanted desperately to get out of the spooky place and get back to the farm, where he felt safe. But there was no turning back, he was here and would have to make the best of it, what ever happened.

"The curtain seemed to be hiding something jolly big behind it"

"As you are taller than Benjamin and me," said the Leader, "will you please pull this curtain down from the pole and then we can all see what's behind it."

Why me? thought William, why should I always have to do the dirty jobs? But he answered, "OK," and stepped forward, stretching out both hands to get a firm grip of the fragile looking curtain, as near to the top as possible. "Here goes," and he gave it an almighty tug.

It was so frail and delicate that the grasses and reeds crumbled as he touched them and fell to the floor in a heap of rising dust. It happened so quickly that he and the others standing near to it had to jump back as they were covered in a cloud of fine grey dust and debris. It made Lucy cough and splutter and she got out her hanky to stop it getting up her nose.

"Look at this!" cried Benjamin in wonderment, as he shone the torch beam where the curtain had been a few moments before. There in front of them was a large, magnificent wooden machine, bigger than William had ever seen in his life. It was awe inspiring to the onlookers, even though it was covered in years and years of grey dust.

"Wow!" he gasped, "Its fantastic! It's huge!"

The others stood and stared in amazement at the contraption as the torch moved from side to side and up and down, picking out its shape and enormity.

"I wish we had brought more torches with us," said Benjamin in a hushed voice.

"So do I," whispered Lucy and she wondered why they were speaking so quietly. "It's not a church you know," she retorted, having eventually clearing the dust from her throat. "Anyway, is this it?" she asked, brushing dust from her hair and clothes. It was too dark for her to really see the entire machine and to be quite honest, machines don't really interest girls, but she had to show willing now that she was here. It was obvious from William's tone of voice she knew it must be something very special, important enough to get him so excited.

"It's our light making machine," said the Leader proudly as he took hold of William's arm and led him forward into the vast room that contained the wooden machine. It stood in the centre of the chamber on huge blocks of rough-cut timber. It was at least five times the height of William. As he got nearer he noticed that the ceiling of the cavern wasn't earth, but was made of layers upon layers of thick woven tree branches, laid criss-cross on top of each other. And the walls were constructed in just the same way he noticed. Why? he wondered.

"Look Lucy," William shouted, pointing to the walls and ceiling. "This isn't a cavern or even an underground chamber, it's like Mr Grundy's Dutch Barn. It's been made by humans a long time ago."

"Gosh, I wonder why? I wonder who made it then?" she asked aloud to no one in particular.

"We did," said a voice, behind them. They had completely forgotten that there were others with them looking at this strange contraption. "We made the ceilings and the walls."

To everyone's surprise the answer had come from the Leader of the Little People, who had been standing behind Benjamin and the two children.

"You did?" questioned Benjamin, turning to him and shining his torch onto the Leader's hairy face. "You made it, you really made this huge covered area, why?"

Stepping away from the glare of Benjamin's torch, the Leader began to tell them the story of the machine.

"Where we are now standing, over a thousand human years ago, there used to be a stone quarry. It was busy in the early years and many humans worked in it. Some of the stone from here was used to build Rose Cottage and long before that, the old bridge.

"In those far-off days ..."

"The stone was used for many other human buildings in this part of the countryside. You must remember, this happened a long time before the sailor came to live at the cottage.

"In those far-off days, so our history tells us, our tribe lived deep in the ground, under a huge forest, many many days walk away from this place.

"Our elders have told us that when we became friendly with the sailor, all those generations ago, he invented this machine for us. He built it here in the quarry in the centre of what is now Bluebell Wood, so that no one would ever find it. By the time that the machine was built, the quarry hadn't been used for over a hundred years and no one ever visited it.

"Humans were afraid to come to the wood because of the noises that they heard. The narrow tracks were overgrown and there were stories of strange happenings and sounds at night. It was this that kept humans away."

This suddenly rang a bell with Lucy, and she remembered the stories that Mr Grundy had told them about his youth and when his father was a boy.

"Sadly," the Leader continued, "before he could get our machine working, the sailor went to sea and we never saw him again. The elders of the Little People wisely decided to keep it safe, hoping that one day someone would make it work for us."

William knew they were talking about him. This whole adventure was beginning to take shape in his mind and he started to walk round the machine, staring in amazement at the complexity of it all. It was just waiting to come to life. But would he be able to make it work?

"After all these years the day has now arrived for us," said the Leader emphatically. "We think that William can help us to get this machine to work again.

"You must realise," he continued, "that it was too big for the Little People to move. We are told that it took two years to build the room you see now. Then, having built this room over the machine, our ancestors filled in the quarry and buried it with the machine, leaving just a narrow corridor out to where we live now.

"We have no books, we can't write like humans, but we have long memories, so our history is spoken from one generation to another. Our Leaders recall the stories of our history and the great events to each generation. This is one of my great responsibilities as Leader and that's why I know about this machine and where it has been for the last few hundred years, why it was built and who we should ask to help us make it work.

"Can you imagine how I felt when William told us about exploring the cave? Then seeing the image of the sea chest, finding the sea chest in Rose

Benjamin waited patiently for William to say something ...

Cottage, and finally the ancient maps and drawings. We just knew after all these years that soon our machine would be working and giving us light in our cavern, in our home."

It dawned on Lucy that this was going to be an awesome responsibility for the two of them if they were to satisfy the hopes and aspirations of the Little People. Questions started to rush through her head as the small group stood expectantly in front of them. When would she and William be able to get the machine working. Would it work at all? What would it involve doing? Who could they tell and share this incredible secret with? Who could they get to help them, because the Little People were far too small, even if they wanted to? Would it require spending any money to repair it, or even to buy new bits for it?

All these questions galloped around in her head but she had no answers as she watched William walk round the great wooden machine .

William paused his inspection, turned and looked at the Leader and Benjamin who were patiently waiting for him to say something.

"I'm not sure if I can get this machine working, but I know somebody who could help me. If you let me talk to him about our secret, about Bluebell Wood and the Little People and all the things that have happened to us, he might just believe us and offer to help," he said with an air of confidence.

"Who is this helper?" Benjamin asked, interrupting William in full flow.

"He is my grandfather. He's Papo T He is very clever and understands about machines and electricity, and things like that. I just know that if I show him the plans and then explain to him about this machine, he will help us even though he doesn't believe in magic. I know he will help me, won't he Lucy?" he enquired earnestly.

"Oh yes, I'm sure he will, William. If there are problems you can always get Papo T to help you."

And so it was agreed there and then. A plan was hatched. With the help of the torch, Lucy wrote it down in a small pocket notebook that she always carried with her on occasions like this.

The plan recorded all the things that had to be done:

1. *Before going back to school William would come back, and with the help of Benjamin check the plans and inspect the machine more thoroughly.*
2. *To do his very best to find out what parts of the machine were missing and make a list of the missing parts, and give the list to Mr Grundy, having explained the whole story to him and his wife.*
3. *What was very important was also to ask Mr Grundy to look for all the old bits of machinery that were scattered around Bluebell Wood and place them near to the clearing for when he came back next holiday.*
4. *The Leader of the Little People, with Benjamin's help, will tell all the others what was going to happen and how long it would take.*
5. *Lucy and William would tell Mr Fudge the whole story when they visited him to say good bye before going back to school.*
6. *Lucy with William's help, and maybe Papo's in Lincolnshire, will have to persuade Papo T to help them.*

Everybody now knew what they had to do over the next few days. However, William found it very difficult to concentrate on the thought of going back to school. Luckily, he knew that Lucy would keep his feet on the ground. She would be able to help him so much, and he loved her dearly for that.

There was only a short time left before returning home, in fact, it would be the very next morning. The two of them hurriedly crossed Lower Meadow to the potato field where Mr Fudge was patiently waiting for them. They noticed he had that very special look on his round weather beaten face, as if to say, you have something to tell me, haven't you?

It was another warm day for this time of the year. The ground was dry and they sat at his side on the grass verge between the potato field and the hedge, both recalling the previous day's meeting and the remarkable events that took place in the cavern.

He listened with great interest and without asking any questions as William explained what he had seen in the hidden part of the cavern. Things that were unknown to so many of the Little People, except of course their Leader. He only knew because it had been told to him by the previous Leader.

"Now then you two," Fudge said slowly, after they had completed telling him their story. He stared at William, "Will you be able to make it work for them? Can you both just imagine the effect it will have on their lives if after all these hundreds of years, living in semi-darkness, their home will have light for the first time?"

These thoughts had passed through William's mind on and off all night and had kept him awake for hours. It was such a big responsibility that had been thrust upon his young shoulders.

"If I can get help, Mr Fudge," but before he could continue, the scarecrow interrupted him.

"William, you can do it if you believe you can do it. My young friend if you believe in yourself and your abilities, you will be surprised what you can achieve. Take your time and don't rush things. The Little People have been waiting for hundreds of years. A little longer won't matter to them. Get as much help as you can and never be afraid to ask. That's my advice to you."

"What I was going to say to you, Mr Fudge, is that for the first time since this amazing adventure started I feel relaxed." William was sure that Mr Fudge knew just how he felt and he thought to himself, I can do it. I'll show them just what I can do if I put my mind to it. If I can make those difficult models at home I'm sure I can get that machine in the cavern to work.

Before they said their good byes, Lucy read the list of important jobs that would have to be done. Mr Fudge agreed in principle with their ideas, but wondered whether they could complete them during school time.

"Benjamin and the Leader shouldn't have any trouble with the Little People," he said, but what concerned him most was how Mr and Mrs Grundy would react to these events. Would he really believe that he, Mr Fudge the scarecrow, could understand humans,and that he can talk to them as well? Then there were the Little People, their home, and Benjamin. He had his doubts about it all. It could be too much to ask the elderly farmer and his wife to accept it all, but it had to be done, or should it?

It was decided between the three of them, there and then, that no mention would be made to their two elderly friends until their next visit. Somehow, they would ask Mr Grundy to look for bits of the machine without exactly telling him why. Lucy had a fantastic imagination and was very good at making up imaginary stories, so she will have to do that bit for them.

"What about Papo T?" asked Mr Fudge with a smile on his turnip face.

"No problem there," answered William confidently. "We can get him to help us without him knowing what it's all about."

All the way home to Warwickshire the two of them chatted about their adventure, hardly noticing the countryside slipping past them as the car sped along. They carefully checked the points once again that Lucy had written down in her notebook to make sure that every eventuality had been covered.

They couldn't afford to make a mistake over something as important as this machine. Would they need another list to cover all the little things that had to be completed at home? A list about a list, she thought.

"No, not really William. This main one will do."

There was no reaction from her brother to that last comment and no wonder. All the excitement of the last few weeks had caught up with him and he was exhausted. He lay with his head against the Volvo door, breathing peacefully as the family car drove north on the M5 towards home, Mummy and a hot bath.

There would be other things to occupy their immediate attention. School for instance, then letting their cousins know about their latest adventure in the cavern, and of course ticking off the points in her notebook once they were completed.

The End